VENT

THE FIRST EVER FILL IN THE BLANK READER PARTICIPATION BOOK

LAUGH, THINK, & VENT

OTHER PUBLISHED NOVELS BY ROBERT K. SWISHER JR.

Historical Fiction: Trade and E-book
Published by Sunstone Press
The Land
Fatal Destiny

Contemporary Fiction: Trade and E-book
PUBLISHED BY SUNSTONE PRESS
How Far the Mountain
The Last Narrow Gauge Train Robbery
The Last Day in Paradise
Love Lies Bleeding
The Man From the Mountain

Literary: Out of Print
Published by Samisdat Press - Canada
American Love Story

Young Adult: Trade Only
Published by Echo Press California
The Weaver
Published by Sunstone Press
Only Magic

Humor: Ebook only
Conversations With the Golf God

Released as E-book:
Bob Roosevelt Mystery Series – 4 novels
Hope
How Bridge McCoy Learned to Say I Love you
A Circle Around Forever

Satire: Trade and E-book
Published by Open Talon Press
Vent

Short stories in literary journals, newspaper work, articles in outdoor magazines.

Reviews by Publishers Weekly, Best Sellers, Library Journal, and many others.

VENT

by

Robert K. Swisher Jr.

PUBLISHED BY
OPEN TALON PRESS

EDITED BY: Janice Spina, Deborah Cassidy, Brad C. Walker
FORMATTED BY: Jesse Gordon
COVER CREATOR: Arleigh Johnson
SPECIAL APPRECIATION TO: Lesley Hayes

First edition
Printed in the United States of America

Library of Congress - In Publication Data

Swisher, Robert K, 1947-
Vent: A novel/ by Robert K. Swisher Jr.
Summary: A satirical reader participation novel covering both absurd and pertinent topics.
ISBN 978-0-9979096-0-9
LCN: 2016913298

TABLE OF CONTENTS

Chapter One is very very short....9
Chapter Two is very very long....11

DEDICATION

FOR MY FATHER

EVEN AN OLD SOLDIER KNOWS

THERE ARE TOO MANY WARS.

RIP

CHAPTER ONE

A LETTER TO THE READER

Dear Reader:

Thank you for purchasing a copy of Vent. Vent is a unique and groundbreaking book. Besides being the story of two people accidentally meeting, you will be asked questions that run the gamut from modern world problems, political, to the utterly ridiculous things many people take seriously. Do not fret. This is not a test. With each question you simply circle YES or NO and write your comments on the provided lines.

Because this is a reader participation book let me emphatically state you do not have to write your name, social security number, bank account password, or any personal information in this book. If you have a book that asks for any personal information, gives a P.O. box in either Nigeria, Florida, or New Jersey to mail the book to when you are finished, **BEWARE**, it is a scam – telephone the police immediately and report the issue even though they will not be able to do anything about it anyway – in fact they might be taking a piece of the action.

There are four purposes for this novel. One is to give you an opportunity to vent your frustrations over the happenings in our modern world. Two is to give you the opportunity to laugh without the fear of being embarrassed. Three, you will be able to state or write your personal opinion without being cut off half way through your comment by some obnoxious, loudmouthed idiot who doesn't agree with you. And four, there are scattered pieces of information the mainstream news and various state and federal government agencies do not want you to know that I feel every person should know.

I highly recommend Vent for reading groups. Each question can be easily debated and it might also give you the courage to state ideas you have kept hidden because you are worried people might think you are stupid. There is no need to worry, we are all stupid at one time or another – normally more times than not. For example – look at the people we elect to be our leaders. To be fair I include members of all political parties and persuasions. But, the question is, who elects these idiots?

Out of the goodness of my heart I will warn you that there are some questions in this book that might offend you. Please, if you do get offended, do not say any derogatory remarks about my mother, she is old and had nothing to do with this book. You may e-mail me and call me anything you want. After spending time in a war, been a hippie, a cowboy, married, divorced, and raised three children, I have been called about everything one can be called.

Vent is not intended for children – although in our modern world the bad language that at times I use in the book is in most children's vocabulary by the time they are six. If you let your children go to PG movies, look at the magazine covers by the checkout at the grocery store, watch pro and college football cheerleaders, watch the Oscars, go to the beach or swimming pool, or partake of the nightly news, no child will be introduced to any information that, when they are older, they can use as an excuse as to why they are hooked on Tootsie Rolls and it is your fault their lives are ruined.

Now get ready to laugh, think, and vent.

Sincerely,
Robert K. Swisher Jr.

CHAPTER TWO

Here are three examples of how the questions are asked in this book: Circle your answer and there is a blank provided for you to write your comment.

Do you believe that under the Second Amendment of the Constitution every citizen of the United States should be able to buy a tank? YES...NO...Here is a space for your comment:

____

____

____

Do you think that building a wall between the United States and Mexico will keep illegal immigrants out? YES...NO...A space for your comment:

____

____

____

Do you think a man transformed through modern and expensive plastic surgery should be honored as the woman of the year? YES...NO...A space for your comment:

____

____

____

AND NOW THE STORY BEGINS. THANK YOU FOR YOUR TIME.

It was April the 5th at exactly 5:30 in the afternoon when I first saw Samuel L. Ruthorford Jr. At the time I did not have the slightest inkling of the life changing impact he would have on my life.

A cold mist seeped from the dull lifeless sky from horizon to horizon. I say the sky was a dull lifeless gray from horizon to horizon as more of a joke because, like most big cities when you are at street level, downtown Kansas City has no horizon. The tall buildings steal the majority of the sky except scattered squares, triangles, parallelograms, ovals, and other geometric shapes I have forgotten the name for and truthfully could care less if they have a name or not. My geometry teacher is probably squirming in his grave but geometry has never really been a great help to me. Geometry teachers are excluded from answering this question. Has geometry been a great help to you in your life? YES...NO...no need to explain your answer.

Also: Has algebra ever helped you in your life? YES...NO...

I had not planned on being in Kansas City. Truthfully, I didn't want to be anywhere in the Midwest, not saying the Midwest is not populated with good people, they are the friendliest and biggest hearted people in America. I can attest to this because I lived in the Midwest for many years. But, as I grew older, there was something about oppressive humidity in the summer, soggy wet springs, and cold winters that bothered both my mind and my body.

A question for readers who live in the Midwest: Do you truly like humidity and snow? YES...NO...and a space for your comment:

____

____

____

The main reason I live in Phoenix is because I like the offensive heat of the desert, the absence of humidity, and the lack of snow. It might be the same reasons 90% of the people living in Phoenix are from the Midwest. Where the majority of people born in Phoenix have moved to I have no idea. Here is a blank if you know where the majority of people born in Phoenix have moved to:

____

____

____

Would you have liked to have been born in Hawaii or some other tropical island? YES...NO... If you circled NO I strongly suggest you go see a shrink but here is a blank for you to write where you would have liked to have been born:

____

____

____

I had flown to Kansas City, rented a car, and driven to a small town in southern Iowa to attend the funeral of my last true relative – my grandmother. My parents are still alive and I do not consider them relatives – they are my parents. They consider me the wayward son, which, according to all their friends every family has one so it is really no big thing. One must merely deal with it. If you have a wayward son have you learned how to deal with him? YES...NO...A space for your comment:

____

____

____

If you are a wayward son are you proud of yourself? YES...NO...A space for your wayward comment:

____

____

____

To not be gender indifferent and cause the wrath of women's groups all over the country I will also ask: If you are a wayward daughter are you proud of yourself? YES...NO...and a space for your comment:

____

____

____

I would not have flown from Phoenix to Kansas City, rented a car and driven to Iowa for the funeral of a cousin. A sympathy card would have been mailed – not a religious one, but one stating in one way or another, "You will always be in my heart and thoughts," not mentioning our only correspondence over the past thirty years was a yearly Christmas Card. Mine to them only signed but theirs always included a letter informing me of all the things that had been going on with their lives. I consider myself a moderately caring person, and I hate to say it, but I really have no interest about trips to North Dakota or Florida, if my second cousin May graduated from college or the fact Uncle George caught eight catfish on May 7th and donated them to the Catholic church which had a fish fry with Cole Slaw, Potato Salad, Jell-O Salad with those cute little marshmallows in it, and iced tea all for a mere five bucks. But, don't get me wrong, I like Cole Slaw, Potato Salad, Jell-O Salad with those cute little marshmallows, iced tea, and especially fried catfish – the catfish fried in bacon fat so your cholesterol level goes off the charts and with so much salt sprinkled on it your heart does back flips. What's another six years added to your life if all you are going to do as an old person is piss in your pants, drool, eat baby food, and scream for more pain pills – the little pink ones that make you feel like you can fly and communicate with inanimate objects. Are the little pink pills worth living long enough to be a vegetable: YES...NO...and a blank for your reasoning:

____

____

____

If your answer is YES you had better have good insurance or you will be in a state run home where your main activity will be sitting in a wheel chair gazing blankly out a window while the underpaid staff spends the majority of their time filling out paperwork. For the privilege of being in a state run home the home will take all but $50.00 of your Social Security.

For you people who think you will never get old an average private rest home in the United States costs about $3,000 a month – a really nice one from $4,000 to $5,000. Is $3,000 to $5,000 within the reach of the average American? YES...NO...

Why does it cost so much to die?

My grandmother was born on a farm in southern Iowa and spent her entire life in the same county except when she took a trip to Minnesota, which she didn't like because there were too many mosquitoes and, bless her Catholic heart, down deep she did not really like Protestant Norwegians. She married a farmer and spent her life on a farm cooking, growing a garden, canning everything from beans to pigs feet, killing and plucking enough chickens for fried chicken and chicken and dumplings to make Tyson jealous, yanking my drunk grandfather out of the bar on Saturday night, and raising two kids, one of which died at five years old from the flu, and my father, who, joined the army as soon as he could to get away from the farm. He loved his parents but milking cows, feeding chickens, slopping hogs, and being one with the land was not his cup of tea.

As a side note: The hippies discovered this also. This is why of the original 7,124 communes that sprouted up around the world in the 60's and 70's only about three have survived. Hippies found out that working on a farm got in the way of carving hash pipes, stringing beads, listening to music and, truthfully, they were not into physical labor.

When my grandfather died my grandmother sold the farm and everything on it to a bachelor Mennonite man who was tired of making furniture and heaters and wanted to grow sugar cane and produce his own brand of molasses – organic with no color added. He had it all figured out. He hired 40 undocumented workers who cut and crushed the cane, boiled it, and poured it into bottles that looked like slightly plump Amish Women. But unlike most farmers around the country, especially Texas and California farmers, he paid his undocumented workers a livable wage and let them live in descent accommodations. He called his molasses, Omar's Buggy Delight, and made a deal with the largest organic grocery store chain in America, and yes, his Molasses has made him a rich man - so rich every 18 year old Mennonite girl in the surrounding area hopes to marry him. But, as with people who get rich and lose touch with the real world, Omar was considering marrying a Lutheran girl – they are hard workers and believe in birth control.

Here is a question: Do you or do you not believe in birth control. YES...NO...and here is a blank for you to explain your answer:

____

____

____

Is oral sex birth control? YES...NO...and a blank for your reasoning:

____

____

____

Another question: What are we going to do when the population of the Earth reaches Earth's capacity to feed and water mankind? Here are three answers off the top of my head. STERILIZATION, NO SEX, THE ENTIRE WORLD WILL COME OUT OF THE CLOSET. God will take care of us is not an answer:

____

____

____

Another question: Is it really other people's business, including the government, what an individual does with their own body? YES...NO...and a blank for your comments:

____

____

____

After selling the farm my grandmother bought a one bedroom house in a small town, population 1,600, and lived out the rest of her days. She loved living in town and not being surrounded by the smell of manure and the fact there was 'Meals on Wheels' and other elderly people she could talk to. The town is called Corydon, famous for the fact in the 1871 the sly Jesse James and his boys rode up from Missouri and besides robbing the bank went to the church and robbed all the people attending the service, leaving all the hard working farmers destitute, but adding to the glorious legacy of a thief and murderer. Who cares if old Jesse killed a lot of people, didn't work a day in his life, couldn't get over the fact the north had kicked his ass, slavery was not a constitutional right, and he left a path of rape and destruction wherever he went, hell, old Jesse was a good old boy, a little mixed up, but aren't we all. Like my father he didn't want to work on a farm and it was before hippies when he could have made a living selling pot to his friends. Here is a question and a blank for your answer. Why are most people infatuated by murderers, outlaws, gangsters, and such?

____

____

____

If you have had a relative murdered, robbed, or raped, have had to pay protection money, had your house or place of business robbed, or car stolen, do you think murderers, outlaws, and gangsters are good people? YES...NO...And a blank for your comments.

___

___

___

What if Jesse James had stolen all of your money from the bank would you want to hang him if you caught him? YES...NO...Or would you have not given a hoot if somebody shot him in the back of the head? YES...NO...

If YES...why?

___

___

___

If NO...why?

___

___

___

Do you think that capital punishment really deters crime? YES...NO...Why for either answer:

____

____

____

There was little to do to settle the estate. My grandmother left her possessions to the Catholic Church – the house, a 1988 Buick with only 32,000 miles on it, canning jars, a few old pots and pans, photographs of unknown relatives, dresses, shoes, winter boots, coats, two shotguns that had been my grandfather's, and $1,492.25. Where the rest of the money she made from selling the farm is anyone's guess, but my guess is it went to buying bingo cards for the Our Lady of Salvation's bingo games every Friday evening where bingo winners were paid off with donated jellies, jams, knitted sweaters, pot holders, Saint Christopher medals, plastic beaded rosaries, and things of that nature.

Here is another question. Should churches have to pay taxes? They all seem to be doing rather well. You may circle your answer: YES...NO... And a blank to explain your position:

____

____

____

If you believe a church should not have to pay taxes should we all start a small congregation? YES...NO... After all you can become a certified preacher over the internet in about twenty minutes for a little less than fifty bucks: Do you think this is right? YES...NO...and a blank for your reasoning:

____

____

____

Before the service started Father Mitch announced that the meal after the ceremony would be in the basement and to please not block the entrance as the ham had not been delivered yet. Why is it that funerals are always followed by large meals?

____

____

____

One would think that a meal after a funeral, out of respect for the deceased, would be a small meal or even a snack. Is my reasoning out of line? YES...NO...and a blank:

____

____

____

When people look back on funerals do they in all truth only want to talk about the food? "Remember Uncle Joe's funeral, best damn apple pie I'd eaten in years. Sure beat the hell out of your mother's funeral. The meatloaf tasted like dog food." YES...NO...

The funeral service itself was not a somber affair. When a person is 96 years old everyone expects them to die and there was no doubt my grandmother was going straight to Heaven – no side trip bus ride to purgatory for my Grandma – no sir, about the only thing she might have done wrong in her life was eat a pork chop on Friday, which, for her transgression she would have said five Our Fathers, two Acts of Contrition, and volunteered to bake sixteen pies from apple to strawberry for the pie sale during Easter – one special pie – gooseberry, for the sole consumption by Father Mitch, who, by chance, had listened to her confession.

Gooseberry pie by the way is both tart and sweet at the same time and delicious with a scoop of vanilla ice cream on top. It is a Midwest specialty like fry bread is to the Indians in New Mexico and Arizona, shredded beef tacos to Mexicans, collard greens to African Americans in the south, black beans and rice to Colombians, curry to people from India, rice to every race of Oriental, poi to Hawaiians, grubs to isolated tribes in the Amazon, pot brownies to Rastafarians, and on and on and on and on. Here is a blank for any and all ethnic groups that I did not mention their traditional food so they can add what their traditional food is. I don't want anyone, anybody, any race, or mixed race to feel left out and try to sue me for being inconsiderate:

____

____

____

Here is a question: Is there such a thing as reverse discrimination? YES…NO…And a blank for your reasoning:

____

____

____

And? Will there always be discrimination? YES…NO…

Here is a blank to list a few of the races that don't like each other: Example: Russians and Polish, Vietnamese and Cambodians, Texas and Louisiana:

___

___

___

I know there are people of all races that like people of other races but are there any two races that really and truly like each other? YES...NO...If there are, list a few. I can't think of any:

___

___

___

Will all humans one day love each other and everyone be equal? While we are alive not dead. YES...NO…

___

___

___

Did you know that before the Civil War many free Blacks owned slaves? YES...NO...

Did you know that in Africa well into the late 1800's slavery was a common practice? YES...NO...

Did you know that most races at one time or another in history have been slaves? YES...NO...

The Vikings' main source of income was selling people into slavery.

Did you know that in many African countries and Arab nations slavery is still practiced? YES...NO...

Did you know that in the so called religious center of the world, India, the people in the bottom caste are treated as little more than beasts of burden? YES...NO...

Just for your information the good old Brits enslaved hundreds of thousands of Irish and sent them to their plantations in South America. This also happened in the early United States but the slaves were called INDENTURED SERVANTS: Did you know this? YES...NO...

A person's color or race has nothing to do with the following question: Is the modern slave a person working for minimum wage? YES...NO...a blank for your comment:

____

____

____

If minimum wage earners are not slaves what are they?

____

____

____

During the funeral I thought about the times my parents sent me back to the farm during summer vacation. It was nice for a kid. I fished the pond for bullheads and bass. I learned how to drive a tractor. I stole my grandfather's cigarettes and smoked them behind the barn. I went to the county fair. I became friends with the Mennonite kids down the road. I helped weed the garden and feed the chickens. I got paid for my work and purchased every young boy's dream - a BB gun. My grandmother hated Blue Jays because they ate the cherries from her cherry tree and were so mean they didn't build their own nests, but pushed the eggs out of other birds nest, laid their own eggs, and took off happier than a lark never having to experience the rigors of raising children.

With my grandmother's blessing I shot as many Blue Jays as I could. When my grandmother or grandfather wasn't looking I also shot the pigs and chickens with my BB gun. It did not kill them, but the various grunts from pigs and the squawks from chickens running around erratically after getting hit in the ass with a BB was for a young mind, funny and amusing. Now it seems sad and cruel, but I am growing old and sentimental and mentally trying to make up for my transgressions.

Question: If you are not a Catholic can you make up for your transgressions or are you just stuck with your past? YES...NO...

____

____

____

If your answer was NO I guess every member of all religions are headed for hell.

Do you think I will go to hell for shooting poor defenseless pigs and chickens with a BB gun when I was a kid and thinking it was funny? YES...NO...

Do you think I will go to hell for killing Blue Jays for no other reason than they ate cherries and don't like children? YES...NO...

Whenever I was on the farm I always missed the city. The farm was nice, but I knew I was a city kid. Strange, during the funeral I missed the farm. Question: Why do we always seem to want to be somewhere we are not?

____

____

____

And, if we really want to be somewhere else why in the hell don't we just go?

____

____

____

Is it worth spending one's life doing what you do not want to do? YES...NO... MAYBE. No blank this is more of a personal thinking question that has to be worked out in one's own mind.

After I got out of the army I only visited my Grandparents twice over the next 40 years. Once for my Grandfather's funeral and once on the way back from Chicago to Phoenix after I had been sent to a class on how to sell gold coins over the telephone to elderly people with dementia. I wrote my grandparents often but why I never visited I really don't know. I could use the excuse I was too caught up in trying to make a living but that is no excuse. Is one's source of income a good excuse for ignoring things in life that really matter? YES...NO...

Here is a blank to list a few things that matter more than work:

____

____

____

After the funeral I shook hands with my first, second, third and fourth cousins, who looked at me like I was some kind of freak because I live in a big city, don't grow a garden or have a winter coat. Then we ate. The ham was delicious and thank God it had been delivered – a group of hungry Catholics could have gotten out of hand and raided the Episcopalian Church that was only two blocks away. The green bean casserole was divine, the Jell-0 salad without the little marshmallows slightly depressing, and the ice tea not what I wanted – beer not considered sacred at most religious funerals, excluding Ireland, which seems to have a good grip on how to really put on a good funeral. The majority of Oriental religious funerals with their drum beating and bell ringing and wondering if Grandma is coming back to this world as a cockroach or a dung beetle are definitely the worst. On the other hand even an Oriental funeral is better than getting torched by a river in India that is so polluted they ship in water from the Detroit River to drink. Here is a blank to state how you would like to get buried, but don't tell me you are going to ascend into Heaven surrounded by a cloud of butterflies:

____

____

____

Here is a ridiculous question but one that intrigues me. After all the years of mankind dying is Heaven filled to capacity. YES...NO...and a blank for your reasoning:

____

____

____

How about the housing situation in hell? FULL...NOT FULL...

Also, this is not really a question, but, if there really is reincarnation I suppose we can never solve world population. YES...NO...and a blank:

____

____

____

In which case there is no need for birth control as humanity does not have a snowball's chance in hell of surviving. Is this true or not? YES...NO...

After telling Father Mitch he did a wonderful job, and consoling him on the fact his days of good gooseberry pies were over, I drove out to the country to take one farewell look at the old farm house, which to my dismay had been torn down, and replaced by a sprawling red brick ranch house that should have been in Kansas. Next to it were nice bungalows for illegal workers with Jalapeno pepper plants growing in the flower beds and a metal factory building with **Omar's Buggy Delight** painted on the side in big bold letters. The area for a mile around smelled like burnt sugar. There were over fifty Mennonite girls in the front yard screaming their names and jumping up and down in anticipation of seeing Omar and trying to persuade him to marry one of them and not some heathen Lutheran. I also spied several daughters that, because I had seen them at the funeral, I knew were Catholic.

Does money have a way of corrupting religion? YES...NO...and a blank for your reasoning:

____

____

____

My plan was to get to the airport with plenty of time to return the rental car, get through security, and have a few nine dollar beers with a bunch of weary looking businessmen before my plane whisked me back to Phoenix. On board I might even get lucky and be able to sit next to an attractive middle aged woman and daydream about having an affair with her on a remote tropical island or even a seedy hotel on the wrong side of town that rents by the hour. This question is for both men and women. Has there been at least once in your life you merely wanted to sleep with someone just for the hell of it? YES...NO...

If you answered YES here is a blank to explain why meaningless relationships are so tempting: People 18 and under do not have to answer this question – all your relationships are meaningless – a fact you will discover normally when it is too late:

____

____

____

How many people reading this pine over their high school sweetheart? Circle either: I DO...I DON'T... And, if you got married at 18 are you still married to the same person? YES...NO...

If your answer was YES why are you still married?

____

____

____

If your answer was NO why are you not married? Please no derogatory remarks:

____

____

____

When I left Youngsville the sky was robin's egg blue with a few scattered powder puff clouds that many people profess to see the shapes of human faces, elephants, fish, bears, horses, Zeus, and so on. The clouds only looked like clouds to me until thirty minutes later they became a solid wall of black, angry, twisting and churning thunder clouds that suddenly began dumping rain so heavy it was almost impossible to see the road, making me miss my turn to the airport and end up in downtown Kansas City. Lost, I miraculously found a parking spot in a part of town that was not infested with gangs whose favorite pastime was robbing older crackers who were stupid enough to park in their territory. To be fair and politically correct these gangs include Black gangs, Chinese gangs, Russian gangs, Italian gangs, Vietnamese gangs, Mexican gangs, White gangs, Motorcycle gangs, Korean Gangs. I am leaving a blank here for any gang that feels they have been left out. I don't want to offend your constitutional right to be a gang and not let you be proud of robbery, selling drugs, killing your own people, extortion, and blaming other people for your lot in life: For example, my Great Great Grandfather had a hard life and that is why I joined a gang:

____

____

____

Question: Does what your distant relatives did or went through really have a bearing on what you do? YES...NO...and a blank for your explanation:

____

____

____

Question: Is poverty the only reason for gangs? YES...NO...
What are some other reasons?

____

____

____

Why don't we just round up all gang members, kill them, and solve the problem? A blank for you to write your opinions:

____

____

____

(NOTE FROM AUTHOR AND I TAKE ALL RESPONSIBILITY) If you are a gang member would you please kill more of your own kind and do the rest of the world a favor. Believe me the only person that cares if you get killed is your mother.

In your opinion is the above statement unfeeling? YES...NO...

I waited in the car for the rain to stop, but thanks to my trusty cell phone, which keeps me connected to all things trivial and useless in my life, I was able to reschedule a flight back to Phoenix at ten the next morning for only $129.00 more, and for free, a scolding by the operator, "You should know at your age to consider weather, car wrecks, flat tires, illegal sobriety checks, road construction, and other acts of God into your travel time to the airport."

I apologized from the depths of my heart and told her next time I would take the bus and asked if she wanted to have dinner with me because her voice sounded like a late night 900 number.

She hung up.

People have no sense of humor anymore.

After my divorce, and being informed by my ex-spouse it was my fault she was going out with other men, I have given up on ever finding love again. I do not know if it was or was not my fault my wife started going out with other men. The only question I have is – Why didn't she tell me she wanted a divorce and then go out with other men? Am I in denial or asking a question that cannot be answered? YES...NO... Here is a blank to list why, in your opinion, people go out with other people while they are married and don't have the decency to get divorced first:

____

____

____

I will state that although I have given up on ever finding love again I really do want to be in love. Although, truthfully, falling in love again scares the (Write a word in the blank that you feel is the most appropriate.) ______________ out of me.

Here is a personal question: Which is better? Circle your answer – MARRIAGE, LIVING WITH ANOTHER PERSON, A SERIES OF SHORT TERM RELATIONSHIPS. You could write a novel with your answer so here are several extra lines:

____

____

____

____

____

____

____

The answer to the above question seems to change with age, but I am not going to ask your age as that is considered inconsiderate in our culture. Why is age a bad thing when we all go through it?

____

____

____

Is it because you don't want to look old when you die? YES...NO...

Is it because an eighteen-year-old is smarter than someone who is sixty-five? YES...NO...

The rain was now a drizzle but I was in no hurry to go anywhere. I hate hotels and motels. It's a personal thing and there really is no reason to go into details, unless people making love in the next room, "Yes, yes, no, no, O God, O God", kids screaming or crying, parties that go on all night, loud TV's, a free breakfast that consists of hard boiled eggs, dry cereal, and your choice of coffee or tea and must be eaten before 6:30 in the morning, the rapid spread of bedbugs all over the nation, has something to do with it. Here is a blank to state why you do or don't like staying in hotels or motels. If you are staying in places that are $300 a night or higher there is no need to answer:

____

____

____

I decided when the rain stopped I would look for a place I could get a beer and a sandwich. Ladies clutching umbrellas in every color imaginable and men with only black umbrellas scampered by. The sea of humanity made me think of robots trying to avoid rust. I glanced at my watch. Why I looked at my watch I have no idea. I think it was merely the fact I wanted to know how fast life is passing me by. It sure wasn't the fact I needed to know what time my search for a beer and sandwich would start. Here is a question: Why do most people own a watch when there are clocks everywhere, your cell phone has a clock, and 99 out of 100 people have a watch? Is it really necessary to know how fast we are dying? YES...NO...Here is a blank:

____

____

____

Do people buy a gold watch for the main purpose of knowing what time it is? YES...NO...

How did watches become a symbol that you have succeeded in life?

____

____

____

Does a gold watch make you a better person? YES...NO...or is it simply a more expensive way of reminding yourself how fast you are dying? YES...NO...

It was exactly 5:30 and the rain was a light mist when Samuel L. Ruthorford Jr. rushed by the car. I didn't know at the time it was Samuel L. Ruthorford Jr. If I had known it was him I would have a phone in late night radio show in L.A. telling people their future and advising them to get the hell out of California. For some reason beyond any definition the instant I saw Samuel L. Ruthorford Jr. I was drawn to him. Don't get me wrong it wasn't like seeing a woman and falling instantly in love. I am not gay, or at least I don't think I am, so seeing a man had nothing to do with it. It wasn't like seeing a puppy dog and getting the urge to pick it up and scratch behind its ears. It wasn't like seeing a child and saying happily, "Boy, am I glad I don't have kids." I was immediately drawn to Samuel L. Ruthorford Jr. like a mindless moth is drawn to a 100 watt light bulb that will drive him into a frenzy more exciting than sex, but will also scorch his wings – scorch them so bad the moth, knowing his goose is cooked, will flutter to the ground screaming, "What have I done!!? What have I done!!?" In the morning ants will find the moth and a few more of his stupid buddies and they will carve them up into tiny bite-sized chunks – ants being smart enough to sleep at night and not chase after light bulbs and candle flames and other dangerous objects. They will laugh as they carry the dissected moths to their deep and mysterious hole in the ground – one of the ants saying, "You know, you'd think that through genetic mutation and evolution these stupid moths would figure it out."

"Dumbest creatures I've ever seen in my life," one of his buddies would reply.

"I tell you what," another would say, "That little piece of meat just above their eyes is the best part."

Question: Are people as dumb as moths because, there is no doubt, we spend a lot of our time searching for things that are dangerous: YES...NO...a blank for your reasoning:

___

___

___

Are people as dumb as moths because many of us march off to wars that have nothing to do with the country's security? YES...NO...and a blank for your reasoning:

____

____

____

Samuel L. Ruthorford Jr. was skinny. By skinny I mean he made a scarecrow look fat. His dark blue suit, with out of date wide lapels, seemed to walk itself. His shirt, open at the collar, was faded white. He did not have an umbrella but somehow was not soaking wet. His brown slip-on-shoes were scuffed and he was wearing white socks. Lord, even I know this is a fashion no no. He had salt and pepper mid-length hair and was clean shaven. He had bushy dark brown eyebrows and his eyes were large and so blue they pierced the drab day like blue silver dollars. His mouth, like his eyes, was large, with thin lips that were moving at a rate lips only move at when they are angry. I could not make out what he was saying. His hands and face were so white he could have lived in a cave and his cheek bones were so severe they pointed out like arrow-heads. He was about my age – mid sixties. As he rushed by the car he was waving his arms up and down like he was having an argument with himself, or he was trying to prove gravity wrong, and was going to fly. He dove into the sea of blue, green, orange, pink, black, and mustard colored umbrellas – the umbrellas separating before him, bringing a vision to my mind of Moses parting the Red Sea. Out of curiosity do you believe Moses really parted the Red Sea?

YES...NO...no need for a comment it could start a war.

For a reason that had nothing to do with common sense my motor senses took over and I got out of the car and hurried after the man.

My motor senses aren't exactly one of my strong points. In fact, if the truth be known, I am searching for a strong point in my character and hope to find one before I die and there is no longer any need for strong points. Here is a blank for you to list a few of your strong points. Physical attributes do not count. I'm looking for I'm kind, I'm gracious – stuff like that:

____

____

____

It was a dangerous journey. The skinnier than a scarecrow man, waving his arms up and down, but still unable to defy gravity, did not stop at intersections while the **Do Not Walk** sign was on, but darted between the cars like a rat terrier with a death wish. A few drivers rolled down their window and hollered insults at him but he merely tossed them the finger, hollering back in a high pitched voice that sounded like a parrot with a cracker stuck in his throat, "Eat shit you driver of a polluting machine that is destroying the Earth. Fuck you and everything you stand for," and hurried on.

Here is a question: Since we know that cars, trucks, buses, and such are one of the biggest polluters of our planet why do we drive them?

Is it because we like fighting wars over oil? YES...NO...

Is it because we think car pollution is safer than cigarette smoke? YES...NO...

It would take a lot of cigarettes to make every major city in the world's air as green as it is from cars, trucks and motorcycles.

Is it because we are just stupid and really don't give a rat's ass? YES...NO...

For you environmentally correct people Subarus also pollute. Vehicle pollution kills thousands of people every year, causes cancer, emphysema, and many other diseases. People cannot smoke cigarettes in parks, in front of businesses, in bars, etc. etc. but you can drive by all day spitting out toxic pollutants and no one says a thing. It's a funny world.

Why don't we simply make any vehicle that pollutes illegal? Don't tell me there are not other transportation alternatives or use the excuse "It would not be cost effective" unless you think ruining the environment and breathing dirty air is cost effective? A blank:

___

___

___

I, being basically a man that avoids danger at all costs, except for a stint in the infantry in Vietnam, I was brave then and learned the stupidity of my folly, stopped for the blinking **Do Not Walk** signs. For some reason I look at Do Not Walk signs and think about snipers and suicide bombers. Weird I know but I have a friend who is afraid of feathers – go figure.

Question: Do you ever worry about snipers and suicide bombers where you live? YES...NO...

Did you know that the chances of you being hurt in a terrorist attack in the United States are less than being bitten by a shark if you were to swim in shark infested waters every day of your life? YES...NO...

Do you think that any mid-eastern country that does not like us has the power to invade the United States? YES...NO...

If your answer is YES would it be like Iowa trying to invade the rest of America? YES...NO...

If your answer is No what are we afraid of?

___

___

___

If Iran got a nuclear weapon - to date we have over 7,700 of them - would they be stupid enough to drop one on America? YES...NO...

How about North Korea? When they get an atomic weapon (they will get one) will they be stupid enough to shoot a rocket at the United States? YES...NO...

How long would it take for the United States to completely wipe Iran and North Korea off the face of the earth if they shot a nuclear rocket at us? Circle your answer: 4 HOURS...6 HOURS... HALF A DAY...THIRTY SECONDS. A blank for your own answer:

____

____

____

Why does the government find it so easy to scare the American public? This is not a YES or NO question:

____

____

____

Just for your information did you know that Pakistan has sold weapons to North Korea and Iran? YES...NO...

Is Pakistan really our ally? YES...NO...and why either way:

____

____

____

Even with my hesitations for safety I was able to keep sight of the arm waving man and watched him dart into a red brick bar, which in downtown Kansas City is no big deal as everything is red brick. The bar was named, BILL'S BAR. I liked the name – simple and direct. It was not complicated like most modern bars that try to put into a name some deeper meaning than a place to drink, get shit faced, and try to talk your wife, husband, girlfriend or boyfriend, into going to their place or yours and taking their clothes off. BILL'S BAR, not The Happy Ending, Welcome to My Place, The Do Drop In, Shady Lady, Leave Your Sorrows Behind**,** please? Here is a blank for you to write down a few names of bars that you find utterly ridiculous:

____

____

____

And a blank to write down names of bars that you think are good names:

____

____

____

To be fair – for those of you that don't drink alcohol here is a blank to write down good and bad names for Juice Bars:

____

____

____

I opened the door, which was battleship gray metal, and came face to face with a second wooden door with a hand painted sign on it that stated in big bold letters: **IF YOU WANT TO SMOKE, SMOKE, IT'S NOT THE GOVERNMENT'S BUSINESS. IF YOU DON'T SMOKE AND COME IN AND TRY AND SUE ME I WILL BREAK EVERY BONE IN YOUR BODY. THANK YOU – THE MANAGEMENT. HAVE A NICE DAY. BILL.**

Question: Why aren't some bars allowed to say they are smoking bars and people who don't smoke just stay the hell out? Sorry can't answer this YES or NO.

____

____

____

If you are not a Hell's Angel would you walk into one of their bars? YES...NO...

If your answer was YES you are stupid.

If you are a non-smoker why would you want to go into a smoking bar? A blank for your reasoning:

____

____

____

I thought the sign to BILL'S BAR had a nice touch, creative and all that, and the meaning was clear and to the point – not like many of our government agencies who I feel their main intent is to confuse the general public. Here are a few of our government agencies. Circle the ones you can identify: ADA, AGRICOLA, AHRQ, APHIS, BBG, EA, BIA, BIF, BLM, BVA, CBO, CDC, CEA, CFTC, CRS, DDESS, DEA, DODEA, FCA, FCC, FEMA, FERC, FNS, FSIS, GAO, INTERPOL, ISOO, MBDA,

MIGA, NASS, NATO, NCA, NHTSA, SAMHSA, TA, UNHCR...I bet you could not identify more than five. If you could you must work for the government, which I should add, is a great job with good retirement.

In a report filed by OMB – Office of Management and Budget – the government does not really know how many agencies the American taxpayer is supporting – every list they release has a different number of agencies. This is confirmed by Wikipedia. Is this a sign that maybe something is wrong with our government? YES...NO...

If you were in charge of a company department and did not know how many people worked for you or what they were working on would you get fired? YES...NO...

Are we, the American People, powerless to change anything in the government? YES...NO...

If your answer is YES here is a blank to list a few ways we can change the powers that be:

____

____

____

Here is a nugget of knowledge. The Federal Reserve Bank is not run, owned, or anything else by the government. It is a private bank the the members of the board are kept secret.

A blank for you to guess a few of the people on the board for the Federal Reserve?

____

____

____

Here is a blank to write down what bank that government borrows from? This should be easy:

____

____

____

Do you think most politicians are paid off? YES...NO...

How can there be a DEPARTMENT OF THE TREASURY when we are seventeen trillion dollars and counting in debt? It is not because of aid programs for needy Americans – these are a small percentage of the budget. How about the billions and billions of dollars we give to foreign countries every year? I am sorry people of Detroit that your town has turned to shit and the government cannot loan you any money because they are giving 250 million dollars a year to Afghanistan so they can grow more poppies and embrace democracy. Is this right? YES...NO... List a few reasons of why the country is in debt?

____

____

____

Would you give money to people and nations that do not like Americans? YES...NO... Here is a blank to explain why you would or why you would not:

____

____

____

If this country is so far in debt. And all the countries in Europe are all in debt. And all the countries in South America are all in debt. And all the countries in Africa are all in debt. Where is the money? Do you have any idea who has all the money? Might it be an international company? YES...NO...Here is a blank for you to state who has all the money if all the countries in the world that are in debt?

____

____

____

Do you care about Social Security? YES...NO...WHY?

____

____

____

Did you know that the reason Social Security is in trouble is because the government borrowed from it without asking the American people **AND HAS NOT BOTHERED TO PAY ANY OF THE MONEY BACK**? YES....NO...

Social Security is your own money taken from your check and the people you worked for. The government does not put in a dime. Does the government think we are stupid when they call Social Security an **ENTITLEMENT**? YES...NO...

____

____

____

Since the government borrowed money from Social Security why can't we, the American people, demand that they pay it back with interest? The same usury interest rates they charge for student loans:

____

____

____

The people in congress and the senate could pay us back by cutting their salaries and entitlements. **ENTITLEMENTS**, I may add, that they voted for themselves.

Also, have you ever noticed that when politicians talk about cutting Social Security there is never a word about them stealing from the fund? YES...NO...

Why is this?

____

____

____

Do you know who the first President was to take money from Social Security? YES...NO...If you don't here are a few hints: He was an actor. He got shot. His initials are R.R.

A blank for your answer:

____

____

____

Ever wonder why that no matter the financial state of the union when it comes to pay raises for politicians they are always voted in? Is this right? YES...NO...

Is it really true that since the government treats us like we are stupid that we are stupid? YES...NO...

Is it also true that since the government finds it so easy to scare us that we are beyond stupid? YES...NO...

I have an easy way to force the government to wake up and take notice and maybe not think we are stupid. It does not involve violence or mass demonstrations or countless outcries on Social Media. You will not have to be beaten by strong arm cops whose main purpose is to enforce the will of the government and in all truth could care less about you as a citizen. It is simple. One year everyone in the United States simply does not pay their taxes. Big corporations do not pay taxes so why not the common man? Some people would go to jail, but without taxes, jailers, wardens, cops, soldiers, politicians do not get paid. I bet changes would come. Do you think it would work? YES...NO...and a blank for why or why not:

____

____

____

Do you think people that have been laid off from work are entitled to unemployment? YES...NO...

Are they merely lazy for not being able to find a job when there are not many jobs? YES...NO...

Should we send unemployed Americans to apply for aid to Afghanistan or Iraq or any of the multitudes of countries we die for and support? YES...NO...

Israel is about the size of your thumb when it comes to countries but we send them billions of dollars in aid every year. Do you think there are enough rich Jewish people in the world to take care of their own? YES...NO... (Author disclaimer: I am not against any religion. Religions do a good job of hating each other without my help.)

I hate to say it but I think we should feed our own before we worry about the rest of the world. How about you? YES...NO...

Is committing a crime the only way to make a living if one is out of a job? YES...NO...

Or go live with your aging parents or Aunt Lucy. YES...NO...

How would you solve the question of unemployment? Government work camps during the depression did well:

____

____

____

I scrutinized the inside of BILL'S BAR. Surprisingly the inside was clean and bright. There was no jukebox or background music and no pool tables. I like a quiet bar. I don't like music that is so loud my bones vibrate and all conversation is shouting at each other with no idea of what anybody is saying. But maybe people go to loud bars knowing they have nothing worthwhile to say and they can run their head about anything because no one can hear them anyway. Is this true? YES...NO...

The inside of BILL'S BAR was about twenty feet wide and maybe a hundred feet deep. The walls were red brick. The bar itself, all dark highly polished wood with a brass foot rail, extended the entire length of the room. The dozen chairs were dark wood with deep brown leather seats. Along the wall were ten dark wooden tables and chairs with bright red upholstered seats. There were four fans hanging from the ceiling with wicker blades that someone had smuggled in from Jamaica. The red carpet was not stained from spilled drinks or puke. Somewhere there had to be an automatic air freshener because the bar smelled like Lilac bubble bath. Three well dressed, expensively jeweled, and extremely attractive young women were sitting at the bar having mixed drinks and smoking. The smoke did not hang in the air in layers but was swooshed in a straight line toward a ceiling vent like a waterfall going in the wrong direction. Seeing the ladies smoking their delicate filtered cigarettes I had a momentary urge to start smoking again. I started smoking at 14, Camels and Lucky Strikes, continued through the army, Marlboros – I wanted to be a cowboy at the time – that was before I knew cowboys spent half the time cleaning cow shit off of their boots and tipping their hats and saying, "Howdy little lady."

But don't get me wrong I like cowboys. Ranchers make a good living in good years, cowboys themselves don't make squat, but so it goes. They like sitting by a fire at night in worn out jeans and holes in their boots and looking up at the sky muttering to themselves, "I love being broke and working for no benefits as long as I have the stars," which is all well and good until they are 65 and their teeth are falling out, their blood pressure is 185 over 110, and their Social Security check is $500 a month.

Big bosses of all companies (ranchers included) make zillions and the men that make it all possible make barely enough to live on. Question: Is this how it is supposed to be? YES...NO...and, if you were a big boss would you pay your workers barely enough to live on? YES...NO...

None-the-less cowboys love their lives even if most of them end up being over the road truck drivers or working in a feed store. And, without them, chewing tobacco companies, both leaf, and plug, and dip, would go out of business. After all the majority of baseball players now chew gum. Question: Do you think it is kind of stupid that baseball players now chew gum and not tobacco? YES...NO...

Or do you think the threat of mouth cancer really scares them? YES...NO...

I stopped smoking when cigarettes grew out of my budget range. It was either smoking or clothes and clothes won out.

The three women at the bar gave me the once over and quickly went back to their cigarettes and drinks. I took it my mid-length white hair, khaki pants, scuffed brown shoes, a cotton shirt with no tie under a corduroy coat, and a minor beer belly are not on the up and coming pretty business woman's priority list. I fall into the mid-list category – somewhere in between old hippie and the lost poet look. But now even old hippies have fallen into the BMW mental state and most poets are poets because they don't have the energy to write a short story or a novel.

Here is a question for old hippies. Be truthful now, which car is better? Circle the answer. A Volkswagen bug. A BMW. A Subaru. We already know they all pollute so don't go on a guilt trip. And a blank to explain your answer:

And, another question. Is marijuana really medicine? YES...NO...

If your answer was YES, did you start smoking pot to get healthy? YES...NO...

If your answer was NO why did you start smoking pot than for no other reason than to get fucked up? The answer is not to become one with the Buddha. A blank for your reason:

Also, merely for information sake, I had several friends who smoked, in my estimation, close to 500 pounds of pot, ingested enough pot brownies to make a guy from Jamaica sick, and for some reason they died in their sixties. If pot was truly the medicine of all medicines wouldn't you think they would have lived to be at least 485 years old? YES…NO…

Do you think Noah smoked pot? After all he lived for hundreds of years. YES…NO…

If your answer is NO what was he smoking?

If we could find out we would make zillions of dollars before the substance was made illegal whether we called it medicine or not.

The bartender was a big man with a chest the size of an oak cask. He was wearing a white starched shirt with a black bow tie and black slacks. A white towel was draped over his shoulder and his black hair was combed straight back with enough grease his hair shone. His face was so clean he had to shave three times a day. He was chewing on an unlit cigar that was as big around as a quarter. He looked at me with dark piercing eyes that were devoid of mirth and said out of the corner of his mouth, surprisingly, in a friendly and comfortable way, "Come on in. I don't bite." Which I thought was a stupid statement as he didn't look like a dog to me. Here is a blank to list a few things that bite. I will start the list: Snake:

___

___

___

The three women smiled at me in a smirking sort of way. Pretty women have their own smirk when they are putting a man down. It's a 'you'll never touch my cream puff' smirk.

A question for women only. Ladies, is the above statement true or not? YES...NO...and why:

___

___

___

I noticed the man I was infatuated with sitting at the farthest table from the bar, still waving his arms up and down, and talking to himself. I wanted to rush over to him, but fought the urge, and sat three chairs down from the ladies. For some reason the ladies reminded me of women playing a role in a 1940's movie when smoking was in vogue – of course at the time everyone thought smoking was good for you, but, the war had something to do with people being nervous.

The bartender drew a small pitcher of beer and placed it, with a glass, on the bar. "Vent," he called looking at the man in the corner who was still waving his arms and talking to himself.

"Here's your beer."

The man stood, stopped waving his arms, walked to the bar like most people walk, slightly paranoid, got the pitcher and glass, did not say thank you, and went back to his table where he poured a glass of beer, drained it, poured another one, drank half, and started waving his arms up and down again and talking to himself. Question: Are you paranoid? YES...NO... and a blank for the reasons you are or are not:

____

____

____

The bartender stopped in front of me and asked what most bartenders ask, "What would you like?"

I felt like telling him I'd like a hundred thousand dollars and a house on the beach in Bermuda but instead I asked, "What is a good beer that is brewed in Kansas City?"

"Boulevard beer, they make a dark beer and ale, three bucks a glass."

"Can I start a tab?" I asked.

Bill laughed, which at first I took as meaning no, and I started to reach for my billfold where I keep my almost maxed out credit cards. "You can start a tab," Bill said giving me a look that if I tried to skip out on paying he would break not only my knees but a few other bones as well.

"Give me one of each," I replied, wondering if Boulevard beer tasted like a black tar road.

He brought two draft beers in twelve ounce glasses, which I knew he had only poured eleven ounces in (after all we live in a capitalist world and every ounce multiplied by millions is one hell of a profit). He also brought a dish of peanuts, about twice as many peanuts were in the dish that come in a complimentary pack of peanuts on a cheap airline flight, give or take three or four peanuts. To my surprise the beers were good, smooth, and had a great after taste. I am not trying to emulate a wine drinker who can talk about body, fruitiness, aroma, and depth for twelve hour stretches while experiencing the ecstasy of five orgasms. Do you think many people take the ritual of tasting wine a little bit too far? YES...NO... No blank for a reason.

Here is some useless information for you, they have proven that sniffing wine does nothing to enhance the flavor - it only makes you breath through your nose.

The peanuts were soft and stale, but humidity can ruin any peanut in the Midwest unless it lives in a dehumidifier. If they moved to Phoenix they would not have that problem – stupid peanuts anyway.

I was about to finish the second beer and down to one peanut when the ladies got up and started for the door. Standing by the door one of them made a call on her cell phone and within thirty seconds three men entered the bar that could have been in GQ magazine. They were so clean and well dressed their teeth even glowed. The men and women each in turn hugged each other before exiting back to the real world.

It has been proven that getting hugged is great for one's attitude and lowers blood pressure. A little trivia I tossed in for education sake.

A few minutes later a group of three men and two women came in. They were all in a jolly mood – even the odd man out. Question: If you are the odd man or woman out does it make you a not so happy camper? YES...NO...

If your answer was YES...why?

____

____

____

If your answer was NO you are well grounded and there is no need to fill in a blank.

The men were dressed in mid-priced slacks and shirts without ties and the ladies were wearing dresses from the discount rack. My guess is they are office workers. The people the higher ups, during private meetings, call serfs and give a dollar raise to once a year while they get a mere million or two. If the serf gets caught stealing anything he will do at least five years in the joint – the higher up will get six months probation because if he was in jail the entire global economy might go in the tank. Remember boys and girls, if you only get one tiny bit of wisdom from this book make this be it: **IF YOU ARE GOING TO STEAL** get yourself in the top echelon of a bank or corporation. Your chances of going to jail, even if you get caught cleaning four billion dollars for Mexican drug cartels or stealing twenty two billion from the American people, are about one in a hundred. Plus, if it does look like you might have to do some time you can move to South America and run for President or just take the country over and make yourself dictator. You can buy a book explaining the process from the United States Secret Service – sorry – you can't buy it on Amazon, and it is not an e-book, you have to order it directly from the Secret Service. Last time I checked it was $18.95. It is titled "HOW TO STEAL FROM AMERICA AND START YOUR OWN COUNTRY" with a sub-title "GETTING LOW INTEREST LOANS FROM THE FEDERAL RESERVE WHILE LIVING IN BOLIVIA."

Here is a question: Why do white collar criminals normally only get probation?

___

___

___

And another one: Is the legal system only for the rich: YES...NO...and a blank for your reasoning.

I will state that a few rich crooks go to jail, normally the ones who have stolen from other rich people by persuading them to invest in a Ponzi scam. Rich people do not like to get ripped off by other rich people. They prefer to steal from those who work for them by paying lousy wages and figuring out ways to get out of giving benefits. If the rich person had stolen from the government he would have only received probation.

The new arrivals started laughing about something as they pushed two tables together. "Hey Bill, the usual," one of the men called.

The usual being five draw beers which were set on the bar. I take it Bill doesn't deliver. I asked Bill, "Who is that guy sitting by himself in the corner waving his arms up and down?" Which, thinking about it, was a stupid question as I knew his name was Vent because Bill had called him Vent – redundancy always seems to run supreme.

Two Questions: One. Why do we ask stupid questions?

Two: Why are we redundant?

"That's Vent," Bill said. "Don't worry about him he's harmless."

"Why is he called Vent?" I asked, not believing the harmless bit, no one is harmless. We all have canine teeth for a reason.

If humans are meant to live on vegetables or low fat yogurt why do we have canine teeth?

____

____

____

Bill answered my question as calmly as if he was mixing a rum and coke "If you ever sit down and talk to him all he does is vent on any subject that comes up. People finally stopped talking to him and that's why he talks to himself all the time."

"I'll be," I replied.

"He's a writer," Bill went on, "I don't think he has ever sold any books but most writers don't. In fact, most writers don't write anyway they just call themselves writers. It's a better description than calling themselves lost or hopeless."

For all you writers reading this, which you should not be doing unless you are going through writer's block, is it true that you feel lost and hopeless most of the time? YES...NO...A space for comments:

____

____

____

Is it true that most writers over indulge in either drugs or booze? YES...NO...

I only ask because I need an excuse for my drinking.

"Do you think I could talk to Vent?" I asked Bill, also wondering how Bill knew so much about writers unless his closet is filled with unsold manuscripts and several thousand rejection letters.

"Take him a pitcher of beer and he'll talk to anybody, but be warned you won't get many words in if you're really looking for a conversation," Bill said.

I looked at Vent. His pitcher was nearly empty.

"I'd buy a pitcher of what Vent likes," I said.

Bill glanced at me like I didn't know what I was getting into, but everyday all I ever really know is that I am getting into my clothes. The rest is a mystery. Question: Does anyone really know what they are getting into each day? Getting into a car, an elevator, an airplane, your clothes, is not an answer. YES...NO...and a blank to list the things that you know you are getting into:

____

____

____

While Bill filled the pitcher I reminisced about my life. I don't remember much about being a kid except visits to the farm. I was an army brat and went to so many different schools in different parts of the world it takes a calculator to total them. I don't know any of my childhood friends. It is hard to make life-long friends when one travels constantly. After high school I joined the army, went to Vietnam so early there were no hippies yet, and marijuana was something only illegal farm workers, jazz musicians, and Jamaican witch doctors smoked. After the army I went to college on the G.I. Bill and majored in feeling strange, alienated, and paranoid (post dramatic stress disorder had not been discovered so it did not make the disability list – my luck.) I have a failed marriage, one child that I let down, one that loves me, and one that does not communicate because she doesn't have the few minutes it would take to call in-between counting her money. Over the years I have held at least eight hundred and ninety-two jobs. Here is a small portion: Store clerk, dishwasher, shoe salesman, door to door vacuum cleaner salesman, combine operator on wheat harvest crews, truck driver, the guy who drives the cart and picks up golf balls at a driving range, adjustable bed salesman, milk truck driver, bartender (at least fifty times), waiter (at least thirty times), pot dealer when pot dealers thought they were Robin Hood or at least mini rock stars and before dealers became murderers and thieves and wanted to own Peru, mowed yards, shoveled snow, worked on farms, ran an art gallery, cut and sold firewood, worked at a pork sausage plant, fishing guide, magazine salesman, all night convenience store clerk that was robbed twice, stood on corners holding signs for tax preparers, pawn shops, and a doggie care center, parked cars, delivered pizza, cooked donuts in a donut shop, washed cars, and many more. Here is a blank so you can list jobs that you were paid a fair wage: It is a short blank because I do not know of many good low paying jobs:

____

____

____

Can a person live on minimum wage? YES...NO...

Can a family of four, with both parents working for minimum wage really say they are living the American dream? YES...NO...

Is a poor person only poor because he or she is stupid? YES...NO...

I know some cities pay a higher minimum wage, for example, Santa Fe, New Mexico pays $10.00, but, most things in Santa Fe are so expensive ten bucks won't get you a beer – go figure? Seattle and other cities are slowly raising the minimum wage to $15.00.

Do most people working at a minimum wage job expect to buy a mansion? YES...NO...

Should people working for a minimum wage at least be able to buy food and pay rent without living on Food Stamps? YES...NO...

If your answer is NO what should they do?

____

____

____

I am currently a car salesman and staying true to capitalism I will use any deceit I can to sell a car. Shame on me but paying rent and eating is important. To be fair to all car dealerships around the country I will not mention the name of the company I work for. I will say the cars are Japanese in origin, some are built in America, some in France, the company is not KIA or HONDA, and until they were made American cars were terrible and built with planned obsolescence in mind. If you do not know what planned obsolescence is look it up. American cars are now good cars only because they had to get better or go bankrupt.

As a side note I tried being a hippie for a year after my college career but it didn't work out – something about lice and crabs and people dying from overdoses quelled the peace and love thing. I also like women who shave their legs and armpits. Does this make me a male chauvinist pig? YES...NO... I did like the no bra movement that was going on but now women who wear dresses cut down to their belly button or bikinis the size of three stamps get pissed when I don't look them in the eyes. I am trying to look women in their eyes when they are wearing a bikini that is no larger than three postage stamps or a dress with cleavage down to their belly button, really, I am, but I must confess, it really hasn't worked – so, if all you women with cleavage down to your belly button and who wear swimsuits that are only three postage stamps would wear a sign stating, **"I WILL NOT BE OFFENDED IF YOU DON'T LOOK IN MY EYES,"** I would be very appreciative.

I will say to all the ladies if you want to look at my crotch and not into my eyes I will not be offended. I know you look at men's butts. Is this sexist or not? YES...NO...and WHY?

____

____

____

Question: Do women dress for men or do they dress for other women? Circle your answer. MEN...WOMEN...

Question: Do men dress for men or for women? Gay men are excluded from this question: Circle your answer. MEN...WOMEN...

But to be fair this question is for gay and lesbian couples. Do you dress for your partner or other men or women? PARTNER...OTHER MEN OR WOMEN...

Also, why is it men don't care if women only want them for their bodies? Because all men are male chauvinist pigs is not an answer:

____

____

____

If you live in San Francisco you do not have to answer the next question. Would it be appropriate if men wore clothes that exposed half of their penis? YES...NO...If your answer is NO why not?

____

____

____

Wait and see, in the near future, when the stars are showboating for the camera before the Oscars I bet there will be a lady with most of her breasts hanging out and a man with 1/2 of his penis hanging out wrapped in a red or blue ribbon.

The one nice thing about all my various jobs is I met many interesting people. I have paid my taxes and Social Security and when I am 66 I will get around $1200 a month. With my luck the government will then decide to cut Social Security because they will need more money to start another war in some backward country that is mostly illiterate, the majority of the people hate Americans and could care less about democracy. If this happens about the only intelligent thing for me to do will be to grow marijuana. It is a proven fact people over 50 have a difficult time finding a job. Being older and wiser I will grow pot in a state where it is legal and take it to an illegal state where I can undercut the market. Capitalism teaches one many tricks – most of which are not nice.

Bill placed the pitcher and two glasses on the bar. "It's on your tab," he said in such a way I knew without a doubt people with any amount of intelligence do not walk out and not pay their tab.

If you ran up a tab at any establishment and the manager outweighed you by 50 pounds, had arm muscles as big as your leg, would you even think about trying to skip the tab, especially if there was only one way in and out? YES...NO...If you answered

YES there is no need to leave a blank for your comments as you are not long for this world.

Pitcher and glass in hand I walked tentatively toward Vent. Vent, seeing me, stopped waving his arms up and down and gave me a puzzled look like, 'who gives favors in this life without a catch?' I held up the pitcher in a gesture 'this is for you and me' and smiled, and he stood, pulled out the chair for me to sit down like a waiter at a five star restaurant where appetizers start at fifty bucks, the entrees are at least a hundred bucks and wouldn't fill up a five year old kid with an eating disorder, the water comes in a bottle with a name on it a French man can't even pronounce, and the napkins have so much starch in them they could be shirt collars. Not to mention the fact a simple gin and tonic is $18.95 because their gin is made especially for them by Brits who pick the Juniper berries by hand and have a Master's Degree in Over the Hill World Powers.

Lord, over the hill world powers anyway, it shouldn't be, "God Save the Queen," it should be, "God Save Us from the Queen." Do you really care how many children British Royalty have? YES...NO...

"Don't just sit there and look stupid, pour us a beer," were the first words Samuel L. Ruthorford Jr. said to me in a voice that reminded me of an English college professor who spoke such perfect grammatical English he was hard to understand.

I knew immediately my moth like instant infatuation to Vent was justified. I also knew scientists who say infatuation is caused by scent are full of shit. If I would have smelled Vent as he dashed by my car waving his arms up and down and muttering to himself it would have been the smell of damp clothes that smelled like dirty pond water. Merely for a diversion I will leave a blank here for you dear readers to list a few of your favorite scents, a few will do:

Vent watched me pour the beer with the same intensity a dog gazes at a bag of his favorite dog treats as his master opens them.

When the beers were poured we looked each other in the eyes, clinked our glasses together and he said, "To destiny and all that other shit we try to make ourselves believe in."

For some reason I replied, "Amen," like the beer would purge my soul, make me one with the universe, enable me to understand the Yen and the Yang, or with the grace of God erase my credit card debt, which, of course, God cannot do. Even he does not have the power to lower the usury interest rate on credit cards that is sanctioned by the government. We chugged the beer like it was the elixir for eternal life.

Quick statement: You can get a mob loan for 18%. Most credit cards are 18% to 25%.

Which one would you get in a tight pinch if you couldn't pay? Circle one. MOB...CREDIT CARD...

And here is a question that is beyond me. A car title loan company charges between 100% and 300% and the government doesn't care. That means a loan you take out for 500 bucks if you are late with a payment will cost you two or three grand. Question: Who owns them? Circle your answer: THE GOVERNMENT...THE FEDERAL RESERVE...BENNY FROM UPSTATE NEW YORK...

Nothing to do with loans but do you believe in destiny? For example - you met the person you are married to, living with, or whatever, because it was destiny. YES...NO...

Was World War II destiny? YES...NO...

The Korean War? YES...NO...

The Vietnam War? YES...NO...

The wars in the Middle East? YES...NO...

If you have been divorced was your divorce destiny? YES...NO...

A blank to explain why or why you do not believe in destiny:

____

____

____

Do you believe in Karma? YES...NO...

If there is such a thing as Karma why were 7,000,000 Jewish people killed by the Germans?

____

____

____

If there is Karma why were over 2,000,000 people killed by the Khmer Rouge in Cambodia?

____

____

____

If there is Karma why do young children get cancer?

____

____

____

Samuel L. Ruthorford Jr., who I still did not know was Samuel L. Ruthorford Jr., showing no social graces, poured us two more beers. I was the one who bought the pitcher and it should have been my place to pour the beers, but since modern society does not seem to really care about social graces I let it slide. Then Samuel L. Ruthorford Jr. scrutinized me in a way I had never been scrutinized before and said in a not so friendly tone, "And what, kind beer buying sir, in the hell do you want?"

How could I say I saw you flapping your arms in a vain attempt to defy gravity and I was drawn to you for reasons or a reason I really do not understand without sounding like a fool so I said nothing and took another swig of my beer.

Not replying angered Samuel L. Ruthorford Jr. and his blue silver dollar eyes slithered into tiny pinpoints of accusation. "What are you some kind of pervert?" he snarled, which frightened me about as much as an old toothless Chihuahua barking from behind a fence.

I decided to tell him the truth. "You walked by me waving your arms up and down and muttering to yourself, and for some reason I was drawn to you like a stupid moth is drawn to a light bulb, and I followed you here."

"I'll be," he said, his eyes returning to their normal size, and smiling a crooked grin that was somewhere between irony and a smirk, and added, "I like the stupid moth bit."

I smiled.

"Did Bill tell you what they call me?" Samuel L. Ruthorford Jr. asked, narrowing his eyes and looking at me like a prosecuting attorney stares at the jury when he is about to lie his ass off to get a conviction. Here is a fact for your information. There is a new law that prosecuting attorneys cannot be held libel for lying to get a conviction even if the man they lied about is found not guilty after spending twenty to thirty years in jail. The ruling states that not having the ability to lie would hinder the prosecution, and also, if one does not know they are lying, it is not a lie. Is this truly justice? YES...NO...

If a prosecutor lies is he not also a criminal? YES...NO...A blank for your reasoning:

____

____

____

"Your name is Vent," I answered Vent's question.

"My real name is Samuel L. Ruthorford Jr.," he said and held his right hand across the table to shake.

"My name is William Brown," I replied shaking hands.

"Not a very inspiring name," he said, but not in a way he was looking down his nose at me.

"People call me Bill," I said, inspiring name or not inspiring name no big deal to me. What's a name anyway unless it's Kennedy, Rockefeller, Jesus, Buddha, and such? Here is a blank for you to add names that you think are inspiring. Please no actors or actresses or romance writers, and please no kings or queens or duchesses or dukes – anyone born into a position of wealth and power whose ancestors were inbred and got rich by paying lousy wages, killing people who hunted on their land or sending them to Australia are in all truth not inspiring at all:

____

____

____

"You can call me Samuel L. Ruthorford Jr.," Samuel L. Ruthorford Jr. said.

"You can call me Bill," I said.

"No," he replied rather piously, "I will call you William."

I felt like saying, "Then I will call you Sam," but I said, "If that is what you like," which is about as an appeasing statement as one can make. Question: Are we too condescending at times? YES...NO...

Vent drained his beer, poured the last few drops out of the pitcher into his glass, drank, and held the pitcher out to me without saying a word. There are times in life when conversation is not necessary, this was one, I knew he meant 'buy us another pitcher', with the emphasis on 'me' as he had no intention of buying a pitcher even if I had been christened with an inspiring name like Rudolph or Alexander.

"Would you like a clean glass Samuel L. Ruthorford Jr.," I asked.

"Chilled," he replied.

I took the two empty pitchers and two glasses back to the bar. Since Bill did not deliver I figured he also did not clean up tables. "Vent can drink," Bill said, without a thank you for bringing him the dirty glasses and pitcher. He brought me another pitcher and two chilled glasses and said, "If your tab hits fifty bucks you have to pay half before you can add more."

I shrugged my shoulders. "What's fifty bucks anymore?" I stated.

"You're a smart guy even if you're not from Kansas City," Bill said.

How he knew I was not from Kansas City I have no idea, but bartenders know a lot of things about life that most of us don't know, it comes from listening to people cry and bitch all day.

Question: What do you think fifty bucks is anymore? And don't tell me a herd of male deer:

____

____

____

Also, are bartenders smart or do we think they are smart because most of the time we are half pie-eyed when we talk to them? SMART...NO SMARTER THAN WE ARE...

I poured two beers but Vent did not pick up his glass.

Neither Vent nor I said a word. He stared at me. I stared back at him. Thirty seconds passed and I was growing uncomfortable. It was way past the twenty second time frame where most people will blurt out something even if it does not make any sense. Silence in this modern world is unnerving – this is why most people when they go camping have to have a radio blasting or they are under the mistaken impression that deer and bears and squirrels, to name a few wild animals, like to dance or don't like the soothing quiet of nature.

Here is a question for any animals truly living in the wild. Do you like listening to music or the sounds of nature? MUSIC...SOUNDS OF NATURE...

Another question for animals living in the wild. Do you think humans who listen to radios when they camp should have stayed in town? YES...NO...

Finally and much to my relief, Vent asked, "Do you know why they call me Vent?"

"You are angry or frustrated over the majority of things that are going on in the world and our country and you tend to verbalize them to who ever will listen, or if no one will listen, you vent to yourself," I said which I thought was a great statement for capturing the twixt of the question.

"You're damn right!!" Vent hollered and banged his hand on the table so hard I had to grab the glasses from tipping over. "I wake up everyone morning and read the newspaper and everything peeves me off!! The TV news peeves me off!! The radio news peeves me off!!"

After the outburst Vent's breathing was so loud and raspy he sounded like a 94 year old four pack a day smoker who had forgotten his oxygen bottle.

I knew better than to suggest that maybe he needed an anger management class so I asked, "Why?"

Vent looked at me like what I had asked was the stupidest thing he had ever heard when in all reality the simplest question one can ask is 'WHY?'

"Why not?" he stormed. "How can any sane person not be angry?"

I hate it when people ask me two questions in a row. How can one person answer two questions at the same time? Luckily I did not have to answer the question as Vent demanded, "Bring up any topic and I'll demonstrate why people call me Vent."

"Samuel L. Ruthorford Jr.," I started, but he rudely interrupted me before I could finish. "I said topic, not my name."

"Same sex marriages," I blurted out.

Why I asked about same sex marriages I don't know. It just happened. Same sex marriages aren't something I really care about. War, genocide, starvation, are more on my worry list but then I had a momentary blast of weird thoughts – some of them being: I have never seen gay dogs, gay cats, gay elephants, gay Kangaroos, or gay birds, there might be gay monkeys – see, I told you I had a blast of weird thoughts. Here is a blank for a few of your weird thoughts, don't be afraid to write down what you really feel unless you are going to lend this book to a friend of yours:

____

____

____

"Don't get me wrong. I don't care if people are gay or not, but the gay people who want to get married are idiots," Vent shouted while flapping his arms up and down three or four times. "Why is it such a big deal to get married?"

"My first marriage was a total wreck," I answered truthfully and just for clarification like Vent I don't care if people are gay.

"Exactly, over 50% of marriages don't work so why do same sex couples want to get married?"

I started to answer government benefits but was cut off by Vent. "Why don't they just want to live together?" he asked.

I started to answer tax breaks, but was cut off again, even though tax breaks is not entirely true. Did you know that tax breaks really only mean something if you are making six figures? YES...NO...

"If they lived together," Vent went on, "then when it came time to split all they would have to do is leave, adios, good-bye, have a good life. Now they have to get a gay marriage counselor, who might be straight, and really would have no idea what their problems are if they are trying to patch up a bad relationship, and if the relationship cannot be fixed they will have to get a divorce lawyer that it doesn't matter if he is gay or not because he is going to screw them out of their hard earned money anyway!!"

"Maybe they want security," I was able to say.

"Get each other a life insurance policy," Vent said, which seemed so simple it was not really an answer – simple things can be confusing so I did not know what to say. Vent continued, "Many same sex couples say it is their constitutional right to get married. Is there anything in the constitution about men marrying men or women marrying women?" he demanded. Is this statement true or not? YES...NO...

"I have never read the constitution," I replied, feeling stupid, after all I am an American.

"Stupid idiot," he accused me. "Everyone should read the constitution, even if it was written by a bunch of rich people who in all truth really could have cared less about poor people. All they were interested in was control. They didn't think people without land should be able to vote." Did you know this? YES...NO...If your answer is NO does it change your feelings about any of our founding fathers? YES...NO...and a blank:

____

____

____

Also, merely for your knowledge, most people at the time could not read or write. This says a great deal about ignorance is bliss and the government in all truth likes ignorant people.

Have you read the constitution? YES...NO...

I am leaving a blank here for anybody that really wants to read the constitution. It is not a blank for comments, merely a time break to learn something: In fact here are a few extra blanks even though the Constitution is not very long:

____

____

____

____

____

____

____

"But," I stammered at the same time wishing I owned land, "wasn't George Washington telling the truth about cutting down an apple tree and tossing a coin across the Potomac?"

"But!! Hell!!" Vent cursed, obviously not concerned with apple trees or a man who could have been a pitcher in the big leagues. "What if I wanted to marry a horse? Is that my constitutional right? Or how about if I wanted to marry a peacock?"

"That's absurd," I said.

"Exactly," Vent replied. "It's absurd. Let gay people get married and divorced just like everyone else. Let them be as stupid as the rest of married people. Let the gay men and women march up and down the streets in San Francisco wearing leather outfits that barely cover their thumbs and jump up and down for equal rights and say how they have been abused and nobody understands them."

There are many states that have voted in politicians that believe the earth is only 6,000 years old, Christianity is not about charity, and marriage is only between a man and a woman. Here is a blank for you to list a few of these states:

____

____

____

Also...do you believe that the majority of the people in the states you have listed believe that ignorance is bliss? YES...NO...

"We need people who don't use the constitution as an excuse," Vent said. "It is not your constitutional right to get married if you are gay. It is your right as a human being. Dumb fuckers."

Do you really care if gay people get married or not? YES...NO...

If you answered YES does the fact many gay people have gotten married changed your life? YES...NO...If it has – HOW?

____

____

____

Here is a question for all married people – gay or straight. If you had the chance to live your life over again would you get married? YES...NO...if you circled NO here is a blank for your comments as long as your spouse will not read this book:

____

____

____

A question for gay people only. What do you think is the percentage of gay people that want to get married? Circle your answer. 10%...20%...30%... 40%...50%... 60%...70%...80%...

90%. I know for sure 100% of you do not want to get married.

Vent picked up his beer with trembling hands and gulped two large swallows.

I picked up my beer with confused and baffled hands and gulped one large swallow. "Samuel L. Ruthorford Jr.," I said. "Now I fully understand why they call you Vent."

"It all started when I went in the army," he replied in a tone that was almost sad.

"I was in the army from 1965 until 1967," I said.

"Me too," Vent replied looking surprised.

We both finished our beers like it was a deep cleansing potion that would erase bad memories and stupid mistakes. I refilled the glasses which left enough in the pitcher for a half a glass each.

"Were you drafted," Vent asked.

"No, I volunteered for the draft," I said. "I was a Mr. Red White and Blue type of guy that thought America sat on the right hand of God and was the savior to the world. I volunteered for the infantry, did my training, and landed in Vietnam before I could say, 'What the fuck have I done', which I did say many times over the next twelve months."

"I was drafted," Vent said. "I didn't want to go to Vietnam. The idea of killing was not a people skill I desired to learn. I wanted to be a clerk. But no, they made me a rifleman in the 9th Infantry."

"I'll be," I said. "I was a radio operator in the 23rd Infantry."

We shook hands again - brothers in arms and all that. Most of my brothers in arms will tell young people if there is a war in a far away land the United States wants you to go fight in forget it – tell the President and Congress and Senators to go fight the war.

Do you think Vietnam, Korea, Panama, Iraq, Afghanistan were all useless wars and have nothing to do with keeping our country free. YES...NO... and a blank for your reasoning:

____

____

____

I did not list World War II because we were attacked and Germany and Japan were truthfully a threat to our freedom. I use the word freedom as it applied to the United States then, not now, but more on the state of freedom in the United States later in the book.

And, for your continuing education, John Wayne didn't join any armed forces. He knew the movie industry needed male actors so he stayed home and made movies about the war. But, since most people think movies are real I guess that is no big deal.

Question: Do you think movies are real? Documentaries are excluded from this question: YES...NO...Since John Wayne was a war hero in movies does it make his a real hero? YES...NO...or just a bourbon drinking coward for not going to a real war? YES...NO...and a blank for your reasoning:

____

____

____

Should John Wayne have been like other actors and gone to war? There is no way he would have failed the physical: YES...NO...

Do you think children think movies are real? YES...NO...

Do you think the rise in violence in our nation and the world has anything to do with movie, TV, and gaming programs? Since the majority are filled with violence: YES...NO...

If your answer is NO a blank for your reasoning:

____

____

____

Having been in a war I really do not like war movies but that is a personal thing.

"If we would have been smart we could have gone to Canada," I said to Vent, adding, "but at the time I couldn't afford a bus ticket."

"If I was rich I could have bought a farm and claimed a farmer's exemption," Vent said starting to vibrate.

"If we were smart we could have gone to Harvard or Yale," I said, "smart people don't have to fight wars."

Question: If we are all equal - the statement is not intended to be a joke...but, if we are all equal why don't rich people have to fight wars?

____

____

____

Did you know that during the Civil War if you were rich you could send a man in your place – you merely paid him? YES...NO...Is this true freedom? YES...NO...Is this right? YES...NO...Did you know money could also buy rank at the time? YES...NO...

Another nugget of information: George Washington was the equivalent of a modern billionaire. Knowing this, when his men were starving and freezing through the winter why didn't he buy them warm clothes and good tents? Circle one: I DON'T KNOW...HE WAS A RICH BASTARD WHO KNEW TRICKLE DOWN ECONOMICS DOES NOT WORK...HE REALLY DIDN'T CARE ABOUT HIS SOLDIERS.

Was George Washington one of the first 1 per-centers? YES...NO...

And, back to the constitution, name one poor or common man that signed the constitution?

____

____

____

Vent started flapping his arms up and down faster than I had ever seen before. His blue silver dollar eyes seemed to expand and almost take up the majority of his face. "And now," he blurted, "after the war in Afghanistan is 'supposedly' over and we are keeping troops there as advisors. Why do a bunch of people who don't know how to shave and have made a fortune growing poppies and a high grade of marijuana need advisors?"

"The Taliban are there," I said, "and they are our enemies."

"We used to back the mother fucking Taliban when they were fighting the Russians," Vent hollered. "We gave them enough money to rebuild half the slums in America. We gave them so many guns and ammunition the board of the N.R.A. bought vacation homes in the Islands and set up secret bank accounts to clean the money the arms and ammunition companies paid them under the table."

Did you know that we used to fund the Taliban when they were fighting Russia? YES...NO...

Was that a good move on the part United States? YES...NO...

If it was a good move maybe we should fund the cartels in Mexico. What do you think? YES...NO...Or how about Elroy Lincoln who is the leader of the biggest gang in Chicago: YES...NO...

Vent continued hollering. "The Russians couldn't defeat the Taliban. In fact they kicked the Russian's ass. How in all of sanity did we think we could beat them?"

"I don't know," I answered meekly.

"And now that we have only advisors in Afghanistan you watch there will be nothing on the nightly news about what is going on. Face it. Afghanistan was like Vietnam. We accomplished nothing."

Question: Did we accomplish anything in Afghanistan? YES...NO...

If your answer was YES what did we accomplish?

____

____

____

Do you really care about Afghanistan, Syria, Pakistan, Egypt, Iraq, Iran, or any other Middle Eastern countries? YES...NO...

I will also ask, Jewish people are excluded, if you really care what goes on in Israel? YES...NO...

And just for fun do you think we truly live in a democratic society? YES...NO...And several blanks for your reasoning:

____

____

____

How about Iraq and the search for weapons of mass destruction? Did invading Iraq accomplish anything? YES...NO...and a blank for either of your answers:

____

____

____

Do you think the reason the Middle East has gone completely into turmoil is because we fought wars in both Afghanistan and Iraq? YES...NO...

Here is a large blank for you to list all the companies that have made zillions of dollars since we started fighting in Afghanistan and Iraq:

____

____

____

"Vent, what do you think about torture?" I asked since torture and the Middle East seem to go hand in hand.

Vent puffed up like a puffer fish that was about to have a heart attack and blurted out a series of questions. "Do you believe if people torture us we have the right to torture them? YES...NO...and a blank for your reasoning:

____

____

____

"Do you think that during World War II, Korea, Vietnam, Afghanistan, or Iraq the United States tortured captured soldiers?" YES...NO...

"When the police use violence or the threat of violence to gather information is that torture?" YES...NO...If your answer was YES, why?

____

____

____

If your answer was NO, why?

____

____

____

"The United States is one of the few free countries that execute people for various crimes. Is this torture?" YES...NO...

"The United States is also one of the only free world countries to keep people in solitary confinement for years on end? Is this torture?" YES…NO…

Could you live in a 4' by 12' windowless cell for years with no contact with another human being without going crazy even though you get one hour a day in a larger cage to walk around by yourself? YES…NO…

Also: Are land mines torture when armies leave them behind? YES…NO…

Many people in Vietnam to this day are still killed and maimed by land mines.

Vent relaxed, sipped his beer, and grinned at me the way a car salesman smiles at a person who has just bought a new car and thinks they made a good deal. Ladies and gentlemen, boys and girls, no one, let me repeat, no one, beats a car salesman. I should know, as I informed you earlier, I am a car salesman. The person who owns a car lot isn't living in the pricey part of town, driving five imported cars, and pays more for T.V. advertising than half the people in South Dakota make a year because you got a good deal. Please. You were shafted – accept it. But, just in case, here is a blank if you think you got a good deal when you bought your car to leave the car agencies name and phone number as I am in need of a newer car:

____

____

____

I was suddenly hit with a big realization. I had to go to the bathroom. Looking around I saw the door to the restrooms. "I have to go to the restroom," I told Vent.

"You don't have to ask permission," Vent said. "I'm not your mother."

I headed for the restroom wondering why bathrooms are called restrooms. I have never seen a bathroom come equipped with a bed, a hammock, or a cot. In our gender proper world men's bathrooms do have changing tables so loving and caring men can change the baby's diapers while the wife is in the ladies restroom checking her lipstick and proudly telling other women how her husband has discovered his feminine side. But, changing tables are too small for a man to take a nap on, so, once again, where did the term restroom come from? Myself, I go to the restroom to pee, or take a dump, not to rest. Here is a blank space for you to tell me why a bathroom is called a restroom when we do not rest in a bathroom:

____

____

____

And here is a question. Since men's restrooms have changing tables should women's restrooms have prophylactic machines? YES...NO...and a blank:

____

____

____

Should men's restrooms have dispensers for birth control pills? YES...NO...

How about men's restrooms have lady hygiene dispensers? YES...NO...

Do you really care if men and women share the same public bathroom? YES...NO...

Do you find it offensive that men who feel like they are women think they should use the lady's public bathroom? YES...NO...A blank for your reasons:

____

____

____

Do you care if women who feel like they are men think they should use the men's public bathroom? YES...NO... A blank for your reasoning:

____

____

____

In the majority of European countries all the above has been going on for years and there seems to have been no great calamities. BUT, Russia still has laws against gay people, which, for all you gay people should mean you really do not want to put Russia on your list to protest gay rights or bathroom privileges as they will throw you in jail for a very long time.

When I got back from the RESTROOM, Vent stood and headed for the RESTROOM.

I finished my beer, poured the rest of the pitcher in Vent's glass and went to the bar with the empty pitcher. If Vent wanted a chilled glass he could get his own.

Bill did not mention my tab when he handed me a new pitcher. I guess he has grown to trust me.

When I returned to the table Vent had finished his beer, smiled at me because I presume he was impressed by my beer buying ability and then hollered, "So why do we get involved with useless wars?"

"I don't know," I replied truthfully.

He leaned forward in his chair and whispered, "I know." And then sat back looking as satisfied as a cat that had eaten all of the dog's food while the stupid dog was barking at the mailman.

"What do you know?" I asked, which was all I could really say.

"The government needs useless wars to keep us under their thumbs. They need an enemy that in all truth poses no real threat so they can make the common man afraid."

"All countries do the same thing," I said.

"But have you noticed all big countries never pick on anyone their own size anymore? They only pick on tiny countries." Here is a blank to list a large country that has picked on another large country since WWII:

____

____

____

For no reason pertaining to the topic I said, "But, the Taliban destroyed the World Trade Center."

"Then we should have bombed them into oblivion," Vent replied. "We should have killed their wives, their kids, their pets. Every camp, every town that hid them we should have turned into dust, no matter if it was in Somalia, Pakistan, the Arctic, or Rhode Island, and when the world said that was not nice we could have replied, sorry, had a fit of madness, but now I have no more enemies."

"You can't go around killing a complete population just because a few of them want to kill you," I said.

"Why not?" Vent asked and shrugged his shoulders.

Is it wrong to kill women and children that might grow up to be your enemy? YES...NO...

If your answer was YES who was it that bombed two large towns in Japan that were mostly populated by women and children?

____

____

____

If someone wanted to kill you or a member of your family would you kill them? YES...NO...

Or would you call the cops and let the cops kill them? YES...NO...

But, let me warn you, the cops might kill you by mistake, saying they thought when you reached for your cell phone it was a machine gun and that is why you were shot 96 times.

If you would not kill someone who wants to kill you or your family you had better move to Tibet and in time let the Chinese make you slaves. Did you ever wonder why we did not go to the aid of Tibet, even though we let the Dalai Lama live in a high rise in New York City? Is it because China is a big boy and not some little ignorant country in the Middle East? YES...NO...

Your reasoning:

____

____

____

Question: Does the Taliban and other Islamic radical groups kill women and children? YES...NO...

Do Christian groups in parts of the world kill women and children? YES...NO...

Why do so many religious people kill other religious people?

And yes, it has happened in the United States, many good Protestants had a jolly old time killing Mormons.

Not to forget the hate Protestant America had for Catholics.

No matter your religious beliefs, is your God a killer? YES...NO...

If your God is not a killer why do people kill in God's name?

"I suppose it was Vietnam that made you become what you are today," I said.

"No," Vent replied. "Vietnam did not make me become what I am today. I did that myself. Vietnam made me sad more than anything. It destroyed my trust of any government. It showed me how cruel man can be and it made me feel lost."

"What did you do after Vietnam?" I asked, having experienced the same feelings.

"I became a hippie," Vent replied, like becoming a hippie was like studying for the priesthood or going to medical school.

"I'll be damned," I said, wondering how a person that in all probability had blasted their brain to the far corners of the universe and back could now be filled with so much frustration. If anything one would think he would be a peaceful blob content with listening to old Grateful Dead records or spending his time dreaming about the yearly Burning Man get together in the desert. I did not tell him I also had tried the hippie bit but I was not a good hippie as I thought the Grateful Dead sucked – in my mind dying from heroin is not exactly the way to enlightenment and folk and rock music will not change the world – although it does make a lot of money.

"It was a noble experiment," Vent said in a tone that reminded me of a certain political figure I saw on TV giving a speech on family values before he was caught cheating on his wife.

A blank as to who you think it was. There has been more than one in recent times:

"What made you stop being a hippie?" I asked with thoughts running through my mind like – hippies didn't believe in marriage, they didn't pay taxes, they didn't need ten bucks a week for a haircut, hippie women were happy with beaded jewelry and didn't need diamonds and mink coats and thousands of dollars worth of make-up, which, looking back now, would have saved me a lot of money and grief.

Here is a blank to list the things modern women want that hippie women did not want?

I am sorry I cannot ask old hippie men the same question as hippie men are like all men. We all want the same thing.

"I stopped being a hippie because it became disappointing," Vent said sadly.

"They had some good ideas that have taken a foothold in the modern world," I said.

"What?" Vent asked.

"Organic food, solar power, problems with the environment, corporate greed, the slaughter of whales, are a few things the hippies brought to the public's attention to," I said.

"They all drove cars," Vent said vehemently, as his arms twitched slightly. "As I said before, anyone that drives a car has no right to bitch about how we are destroying the environment, like anyone that wears leather shoes has no right to complain about animal cruelty."

"But they are noble causes," I said.

"Noble causes need noble people to pursue them," Vent stated.

Here is a blank to write down a few noble hippies if you are old enough to remember the sixties, or lived through them and can still remember anything. Neither Timothy Leary nor any of the Beatles could be called hippies, so scratch them from your list – also no folk singers that now reside in million dollar homes in Malibu:

____

____

____

Here is a blank for those born in the 70's to the present to write down people they feel are noble. Jimmy Buffet, The Black Eyed Peas, Reagan, Clinton, and any of the Bush family do not count nor any of the Star Wars characters:

____

____

____

Vent suddenly started flapping his arms furiously up and down, back to the old let's try and beat gravity bit, jumped up from the table, and hollered at the top of his lungs, "And the environment debate really, really, really, pisses me off."

Not one customer in the bar bothered to look over at Vent, reminding me of reports I have heard about people getting beat up in New York City while 100,000 people walk by without helping. Good old New York City, Mecca of the United States, where you only have to have sixteen locks on your door to keep the thieves out and rent is so high sixty grand a year will allow you to live in the slums. But everything has a good side, bagels and pizzas are cheap. I must warn you though if you are a minority beware of the cops.

Is one reason cops seem to pick on minorities the fact most minorities cannot afford to hire good lawyers? YES...NO...

Or is it minorities are nothing but criminals? YES...NO...

Question: Is New York City really all that good? YES...NO...

Or how about L.A? YES...NO...

Detroit and Chicago have more murders every year than any other city in the country. My question is why do people even live there? The only reason I can think of is they don't have enough money to get out. Do you think this is true? YES...NO...

____

____

____

Vent glared at me, my thoughts had taken me away from his rant. "What were you saying about the environment?" I asked with an, 'I am sorry' tone.

Vent drank some beer, sucked in a big breath of bar air, and began. "There are a huge amount of people in the world who cry we are changing the environment and we have to stop what we are doing. Of course we are changing the environment. But, I bet the majority of the people who cry and protest heat their homes with gas, drive cars, wear tennis shoes, which, if they don't know are mostly a petroleum based product, fly in airplanes, have light bulbs in their houses using electricity generated from coal fueled power plants." Vent stopped to take another deep breath. Even I know the list is endless, so while Vent was deep breathing, I asked, "So?"

"So, so," Vent hollered. "So if you partake of the monster you have no right to bitch.

We can solve the present problems simply by not heating our houses with gas or electricity. Stop driving cars, trucks, farm machinery, motor boats or anything with a gasoline or diesel fuel combustion engine. Stop using oil based fertilizers."

"If people heated with wood there would be no trees left," I said.

"True."

"If we didn't use oil based fertilizers we would all starve," I said.

"True."

"The climate has always changed," I said. "We are changing it for sure but climate is not static."

"True. There are fish fossils on the tops of mountains. The Sahara Desert used to be a big lake. There are fossilized trees in the desert. All the land masses on Earth today were at one time one land mass and in time will be one land mass again."

"What are we going to do?" I asked, trying to ignore a deep sense of depression from sliding into my mind like an evil slinky."

"Scientist will figure it out," Vent said nonchalantly. "We might kill off half the animals in the world, wipe out the majority of the human race, destroy all the forests so people can have expensive furniture, pollute the oceans so badly all the fish will have to learn how to fly, but a few people will survive."

"How can you be so calm about it?" I hollered. Hollering has a way of abating depression.

"What else is there to do?" Vent asked. "If I could go back and talk to the dinosaurs, zillions of fossilized fish, saber toothed tigers, woolly mammoths, birds that couldn't fly, trilobites, giant snails, sharks the size of a bus, Neanderthal man, and on and on they might be able to give me a few clues."

I thought. I thought some more. I pondered. I pondered some more. I debated and debated more. I rationalized and rationalized more. My thinking and pondering and debating and rationalizing did not come up with an answer so I shrugged my shoulders.

Do you think or don't think shrugging one's shoulders is a good solution to the problem?

YES SHRUGGING IS GOOD...NO SHRUGGING IS NOT GOOD.

Do you think the owners of the companies that are the biggest polluters really care if the world is a chemical toxic brew? YES...NO...

Did you know that the electric companies are trying their best to hinder the development of solar power? YES...NO...and why would they do that?

____

____

____

Do you believe that all the toxins we spew into the atmosphere and land has any effect on the environment? YES...NO...

If you circled NO would you drink Round Up? YES...NO...

If you circled NO would you stick your nose into the tail pipe of a car for twenty minutes? YES...NO...

What can be done to control our impact on the environment that big business would agree to? A few lines for your recommendations:

____

____

____

Any good ideas will be sent to all major corporations, all governments, the utility companies, Greenpeace, all the save organizations: save a tree, save an owl, save a minnow, save the ocean, save fish, etc, etc.

Here is another blank for all the save organizations I did not list that want to take a few minutes out of their saving efforts to write the name of your cause: If you leave a link I will post it on my Facebook page and maybe even get a few shares.

____

____

____

Here is a blank space for people to write down a few of the save organizations that are truly ridiculous. I must first write a disclaimer: The opinions stated in the following blank are the opinions of readers and I take no responsibility:

____

____

____

Here also is a blank for people to try and tell me the reason for devastating earthquakes, tornadoes, hurricanes, tidal waves, volcanoes, mud slides, ice ages, hail storms, straight line winds, meteor strikes, all of which kill thousands upon thousands of people, have killed thousands and thousands of people, and will continue to kill thousands and thousands of people and at the same time drastically change the environment. But, and I repeat, but, I will not accept God's Will as an answer:

____

____

____

I hate to say it even though it makes me feel small and insignificant, I do not feel that humans are the center of the universe. Do you think humans are the center of the universe?

YES...NO...Why for either answer:

____

____

____

Here is a morbid question. If all of mankind decided mass suicide was the only answer to global warming and the best way to save the planet would the Earth be a better place? YES.....NO...

And if we did commit mass suicide would dolphins and elephants and horses and every other living creature on the face of the Earth really care? YES...NO...

Here is a blank for all of you animals that can read to tell us humans if you really care if we commit mass suicide or not:

And, because many people believe the Earth is a living breathing entity, do you think the Earth really cares if mankind would wipe itself out? YES...NO...

"So besides disappointment what else made you stop being a hippie?" I asked Vent. I was tired of natural disasters and the environment, but I did have a strange thought. I wondered how much energy is wasted every year producing beer and I had another strange thought. The thought being: is there a group that wants to save hops? Can you imagine? People walking around breweries chanting, "No beer, the process is ruining the environment and killing hops." But, to add to the weird thought, I bet people who love wine and protested the bad treatment of hops could care less about all the pain and agony they put grapes through, lord, hops merely get cooked, poor grapes get stomped on, their skin ripped off and then cooked. Question: Do you feel sorry for either hops or grapes? YES...NO...

It has been proven that plants feel pain. Does this in anyway change your answer to the above Question: YES...NO...I COULD CARE LESS...

If there is a plant reading this book do you feel sorry for hops and grapes? YES...NO...

"If you are a weed reading this book do you think Round Up and other weed killers, even organic weed killers, should be made illegal? YES...NO...

Did you know that many plants we label obnoxious weeds are really nutritious and should be a part of our daily diet? YES...NO... If you answered YES what are a few of them? I will start. Dandelions and thistles:

"I stopped being a hippie because the bottom fell out of the economy," Vent said, answering my question, "and, for your information, I did not do any drugs. I figured if I did drugs my mind would do flip flops and I would start to like bell bottom pants and clothes that didn't match. I hired six illegal aliens from Mexico and set up a small factory in San Jose hand carving peace signs from all kinds of wood. At the time the Border Patrol didn't arrest many illegal aliens. The farmers in California and Texas were making so much money by paying the illegal aliens little or nothing they used the surplus to pay off the Border Patrol cops. Years ago how the farmers treated illegal aliens was called slavery but I don't think the Mexican workers understood the term. I paid my workers $3.00 an hour. The peace symbol business was good. I had peace symbol necklaces, key chains, tie tacks, bracelets, peace symbol pins that ranged in size from a few inches to three feet around and I was working on an idea for peace symbol shoes with springs built into the heels. I had outlets in grocery stores, head shops, flea markets and several off the wall churches that believed in levitation and that Mickey Mouse was the true son of God. I also had people who bought them for a 50% discount and sold them on street corners to support their heroin habit. But, like I said, the bottom fell out. One day you couldn't give a peace symbol away. It was like the hippies had evaporated into space and had accepted the fact there will be wars and smoking copious amounts of pot does not change the world it only gives you black lung. (I interject here. Sorry boys and girls, tar is not good for your lungs, ask some of the old hippies now dying from lung cancer. Don't ask the ones that can't remember their names and only hum all the time.) Vent continued: "So I left California and was accepted into the

University of Texas in Austin where I majored in Creative Writing and really started to get pissed."

"I'll be," I said, not so much about Vent's story but the fact, in the 1970's Vent was generous for paying $3.00 an hour because the minimum wage at the time was $1.60 and the poverty level for a family of three was $3,100.

"I should have majored in business or something practical," he said, "Listening to writing professors telling me when a specific author wrote, 'the train is moving too fast,' the author really meant he wanted to sleep with his grandmother while the dog watched is ludicrous."

Vent's voice raised two octaves. "When a writer says, 'the train is moving too fast,' he means exactly that. I want to shake your hand doesn't mean I want to lick the top of your head. Have a nice day doesn't mean I think you have a nice ass. Where do they come up with all that shit?"

Here dear reader, on behalf of Vent, is a question. Do you think that what a writer writes is exactly what he really means? YES...NO...

If your answer is NO write a statement from this book in the blank below and explain to me what I really meant. It will be a great help because the majority of the time I have no idea what I mean about anything:

____

____

____

"When I am with a woman and she tells me something, I know it is not what she really means," I said.

"No shit," Vent said, like what I said was a universal truth if there really is one, and like all universal truths it cannot really be explained – it is just taken for granted.

To be fair, for all you women here is a blank for you to say the same thing about men, that is, if you think men are smart enough to say something that really has any meaning. For example – if you think men are just full of shit and really don't know what the hell they are saying simply write, YOU BET YOUR BOOTY in this blank:

____

____

____

And here is a blank if by chance you changed your mind about the YOU BET YOUR BOOTY question:

____

____

____

"So what did you do with your creative writing degree?" I asked Vent.

Vent took several deep swallows from his beer, looked at the ceiling, looked at me, and said, "I became a bartender."

I could not help it, I laughed. And Vent, straying from his name said, "Life is absurd and has no meaning," and laughed with me.

And here is a blank for you to write down a few things in life that you think have meaning:

____

____

____

And here is a blank to write down things in life that in one hundred years will have meaning:

____

____

____

Or how about a blank for things in life that will have meaning in one thousand years:

____

____

____

And, what things in life will have meaning in approximately six billion years, give or take a million in either direction, when the sun novas and our little planet becomes space dust?

____

____

____

With blanks to fill in like the ones above I guess should have stayed being a hippie, but sorry to say, I couldn't stand the scent of patchouli oil, which every hippie girl seemed to bathe in, I think it was cheaper than water, and I couldn't get into phrases like, "wow, groovy, far out man, I can dig it, right on," and the first time I tried to roll a joint and become one with the crowd the true hippies laughed at my attempt. The ability to roll a joint was an ego thing, kind of like long hair and beads and how many holes were in your pants. Isn't it strange how non-conformists have to conform? Do you believe it is true that to be a non-conformist you have to conform to your non-conformist group? YES...NO...and a blank to explain why this is not weird:

____

____

____

A true non-conformist cannot belong to any group. YES...NO...

The thing that really made a person high up on the echelon chain of hippiedom was a Volkswagen bus – especially if the top popped up and came equipped with a stove and a sink. Myself, I liked pick-up trucks, not cool, especially if they had a gun rack, and, not being able to role a joint I gave up trying to conform to become a non-conformist – besides pot cost more than tobacco and I had quit smoking after I got out of Vietnam. Cigarettes were free in Nam – one of the benefits of the war. I think doctors at the time lobbied for the tobacco industry, they sure as hell didn't want to see us all well. If we were all well they would have to develop a disease so they could keep charging people ridiculously high prices. Don't believe their line, "Well med school was expensive and took many years of my life and my insurance is expensive, that is why it will cost you most of all the money you have for me to even look at you, and if you don't have insurance don't let the door hit you in the ass as you head down to the county hospital where you will receive terrible care."

Do you think your doctor really cares if you die while he is on his vacation? YES...NO... Disclaimer: There are many caring doctors. They are usually broke and working in a foreign country. There are a few working in our poverty areas and slums.

"Did you write while you were a bartender?" I asked Vent, fed up with my mind darting between hippies and doctors and still slightly miffed that I could never roll a decent looking joint.

"Not much," Vent replied.

"I flunked out of college," I said.

"At least you did not have to take a creative writing class," Vent said, adding, "Bring up another topic I can vent about."

"What do you think about women in the military serving in a combat role?" I asked.

To my surprise Vent did not start flapping his arms. His blue silver dollar eyes did not start to bulge. He merely stated in a calm and collected tone, "I think it is a great idea. Let the women get their arms and legs and feet and breasts and parts of their faces blown off. At least they wouldn't have to worry about having their balls shot off. Their husbands could stay home and take care of the kids. They could learn how to do the laundry, iron, cook, shop at the grocery store, run a vacuum, braid a girl's hair, collect coupons, the right and wrong way to tell a teenage girl when she has her first period that she isn't dying, and things like that. I bet after a few years if you asked a man if he wanted to join the armed forces he'd look at you in disbelief and say, "You have to be kidding. I've got it made. When the kids are in school I play golf. Also, after a few years I know our population would start to go down, dedicated military women couldn't fight wars if they were pregnant."

Do you think it is a good idea that only women be allowed in combat rolls? YES...NO...

____

____

____

Here is a question for men only. If you had your choice of either doing the dishes or going to a combat zone which would you rather do? DISHES...COMBAT ZONE...

____

____

____

Here is another blank for you to put how long you think it would take a pregnant woman to low crawl one hundred yards through the jungle or desert (your choice) loaded down with an ammo belt, a few grenades, knife, flak jacket (especially conformed for women) canteen, a back pack with all the necessary items for combat (food, first aid kit, rain poncho, stuff like that) and a 60 caliber machine gun:

____

____

____

"I also think, as long as we have people in this country who want to spread our will around the world, that everyone, girl and boy, when they reach 18 years old should have to do three years in the military," Vent said.

Do you think every boy and girl when they reach 18 should have to go in the military, this means rich and poor kids – no exemptions for school, farmer, or anything? YES...NO...

And a blank for your comments:

____

____

____

Do you think that if this happened within a few years many of the people who have never been in the military and are always proclaiming we need more troops in foreign countries would change their attitude about war? YES...NO....and your reasoning:

____

____

____

"And what do you think about genetically modifying animals and plants?" I asked Vent.

We had covered the women in the military and mandatory military service topics more than enough.

Vent buried his face in his hands like a little kid covers his face and thinks because he cannot see you, you cannot see him. Strange grunting sounds filtered through the cracks between his fingers. They sounded like the warning grunts from an angry sow when a farmer is approaching her babies. If you have never been around an angry sow let me inform you they are mean and dangerous. A large pig has no qualms about taking big chunks of flesh out of your body, in fact, if you happen to fall down in a pig lot, and cannot get up, the pigs will thoroughly enjoy eating every last bit of you. They especially like bone marrow. This is the main reason I have always liked pork over beef. If a pig will eat me I sure as hell don't feel any guilt about eating him. Oh dear, I forgot, I have to be politically correct – I sure as hell don't feel any guilt about eating him or HER. Cattle on the other hand don't eat meat – go figure. Jewish people will not eat pork when pigs would eat them, but they will eat beef when the cattle only eat green leafy things. Was God confused or did the Jewish people mistakenly think God said pig when He said cattle? They both have split hooves: YES GOD WAS CONFUSED… NO THE JEWISH LEADERS WERE CONFUSED… and a blank

____

____

____

Vent took his hands away from his face. His face was so red it looked like he had been in the sun too long and had forgotten to put on sunscreen. "When the Aztecs were growing corn, bless their little ground to the nub teeth from eating corn ground in a stone basin, an ear of corn was about the size of your thumb, now there are so many varieties of corn you can't count them. Everything has been genetically modified through time: peas, beans, corn, grapefruit, trees, animals, even us, everything, coffee beans, potatoes, oranges, tangerines, nectarines, peaches, almonds, walnuts, cherries, blueberries, strawberries, gooseberries, lettuce, cabbage, onions, and on and on, pigs, cows, chickens, turkeys, fish, and on and on. We live longer because of food that has been genetically modified. Either we breed traits through time into vegetables and animals or we inject genes into them. Is a gene a gene or is a gene not a gene? What's the big deal? I don't understand?"

Question: Is a gene a gene or is a gene not a gene? IS...IS NOT...

"Some people say it could harm us," I said, "and the environment."

"If we can genetically enhance crops for better yields and drought and insect resistance we should at least try. History is dotted with blights and famines caused by insects and droughts that caused millions of people to die from starvation and malnutrition. They can even add vitamins to crops now. Vitamins to the western world really don't mean a lot as most of us are overweight but to a starving population it can mean the difference between life and death."

"Some people say it is only the big agricultural companies that will have control over our food," I said, adding, "and they are only in it for the profit."

"They already have control and isn't everything done for a profit?" Vent screeched, jumped to his feet and flapped his arms up and down faster than I had ever seen before. "Or do all the people work for free that grip about people who work for profit?"

"Will you say that again," I said, more than a little confused.

"No," Vent replied slightly calmer.

Question: Do you work for profit or do you work not to profit? PROFIT...NOT FOR PROFIT...

If you do work for free I am looking for someone to mow my yard, wash my car, and many other tasks around the house and I will gladly not pay you. Not because I am cheap but because I am broke.

Do painters paint in hopes their paintings don't sell? SELL...DON'T SELL...

Do writers write to only collect rejection letters? YES...NO...

Do organic farmers work to not make any money? YES...NO...

Do non-profit companies pay their executives? YES...NO...

The average salary of a non-profit CEO in 2014 was $118,000 with many making over $300,000. This does not count compensation packages.

Do you think this is too much for a CEO of a non-profit to make? CEO's of a non-profit do not have to answer: YES...NO...

If you answered YES what should a CEO of a non-profit get paid?

____

____

____

"To sum it up, about genetically modified food," Vent said emphatically. "If you don't like it don't eat it and just for your information the majority of organic food has been genetically modified. In my opinion many of us are spoiled motherfuckers. Half the stuff we throw in the garbage starving people would kill for. People who gripe about food should stop eating for three months, let their stomach bloat, their hair start to fall out, their teeth get loose, wish they could shit, and then move to Africa with their families and watch their children die and protest that genetically altered food is bad for you."

Are the majority of us truthfully what Vent says "A bunch of spoiled motherfuckers that have never known what hunger really is?" The seven million people living in the United States below the poverty level do not have to reply. YES... NO...

Why, since we are one of the richest countries in the world do we have so many hungry people? Circle one: GREED...NOT CARING...WE ARE REALLY NOT A RELIGIOUS PEOPLE...I DON'T KNOW...

If you were starving would you eat genetically modified food, even if it was bad for you, or would you starve to death? EAT...NOT EAT...

If your answer was NOT EAT can people live on faith alone no matter what your faith is? YES...NO...

If you can live on faith alone does it make good soup? YES...NO...

"Since we are on the subject of food what do you think about pesticide use on food crops?" I asked Vent.

"It is necessary but also overused," Vent said. "There are many ways we can curtail plant diseases without pesticides, but for large scale food production it is not always practical."

Do you agree with this? YES...NO...

"We do use too many antibiotics and growth hormones in the animals we eat," Vent said.

What can we as a people do to try and curtail the use of antibiotics and growth hormones in the production of meat products? Here is a blank:

____

____

____

Is it possible to have enough free range chickens to feed millions of people? YES...NO...

Is it possible to have enough meat production without overcrowding the animals?

YES...NO...

According to several studies there is no dietary difference between organic and non-organic food. Do you believe this? YES...NO...

Why is organic food more expensive when in reality it is cheaper to produce because of the lack of pesticides, inorganic fertilizer, and injections?

____

____

____

Are organic growers really just another greedy capitalistic group that is cashing in on a trend? YES...NO...and a blank:

____

____

____

Can the world grow enough organic food to feed mankind? YES...NO...

Can the world grow enough food of any kind to feed mankind? YES...NO...

If your answer was YES why are so many people around the world starving? War is one answer. Greed is another.

____

____

____

And, to put an end to this subject, since the world is highly polluted (car exhaust, coal exhaust, nuclear waste, every bad chemical known to man in the water including rain water) can there really in all truth be anything grown or bred that is organic? YES...NO...

Do you think lawns should be made illegal because of the water and chemicals that are put on them? YES...NO...

Miracle Grow is a great flower fertilizer and is not organic. Should it be made illegal? YES...NO...

"What about chemical weed killers?" I asked Vent.

"Pull all the weeds by hand," was all he replied.

Is it possible to pull all thc weeds that grow in the millions of acres of vegetables in this country by hand? YES...NO...and a blank:

____

____

____

I think the answer is YES. We could use all the people in jail, all the homeless, all the people out of work, high school and college students, illegal immigrants, and the military when they are not off fighting a war thousands of miles away. Is this unreasonable? YES...NO...

Vent looked at the empty pitcher of beer, looked at me with imploring eyes, which I quickly looked away from. Imploring eyes, in all of my experiences in life, should be avoided at all costs. He then, much to my surprise, picked up the empty pitcher and two glasses and said, "I'll buy this one and unlike you, you rude bastard that did not get chilled glasses the last time, I will get us two chilled glasses."

Question: Was I rude for not getting chilled glasses when I knew I should have gotten chilled glasses? There is only one answer which you may circle: YES...

The question now is, why was I rude:

Am I my brother's keeper, although Vent is not my true brother, we are brothers in the fact we are both human? YES...NO...

Do you care about your brothers and sisters of mankind or could you care less? I CARE...I COULD CARE LESS...

If you care about your brothers and sisters in life do you give beggars money? YES...NO...

Or do you ignore them? YES...NO...

Do you care if people in Africa are starving? YES...NO...

Here are a few nuggets of information. Did you know that the southern states in the United States have a 30% poverty rate, including Texas? YES...NO...

The southern states pay the lowest minimum wage. The southern states do their best to wipe out the unions. They spend less for education. Have the worst healthcare in the country. The most people with bad teeth. The most Evangelical Christians and the most gun owners. The south also has the most violent crime not counting Chicago which is in a world of its own. Does this mean that as long as people believe in God, have a gun, don't care if they eat or not, don't care about good health care or having a job, everything is fine? YES...NO...and a blank for any comment:

Does being poor, being religious, having a gun, and no job, have anything to do with freedom? YES...NO...

I am neither a Republican nor a Democrat but the majority of governors from the south are Republican. But, to be fair, during the worst part of segregation the majority of governors in the south were Democrats. But, not wanting to get into a history of either party, the parties have completely turned around in their beliefs from years ago. If you do not believe this go to the library and do some research. Do you think I am lying? YES...NO...Why would I lie?

Watching Vent walk toward the bar I was slightly peeved. Vent had called me a bastard and I am not a bastard. My parents were married when I was born, or at least I have been told they were. Bastards did do good in medieval Europe when their father was a king or at least a duke and neither of whom really cared about feeding the poor with any kind of food – genetically altered or not. In fact, taxes for the poor were the majority of the poor people's crops, which enabled the kings and dukes to have big feasts with lots of wine and create bastards with serving girls while the poor got rickets and had an average life expectancy of twenty-eight years. And, sorry to say, Robin Hood did not have enough clout to really make much of a difference, unless you were one of his merry men and got to share in the spoils. Poncho Villa pulled off the same trick in Mexico. Can you believe that peasants really think that people trying to overthrow a government really care about them? I am leaving a blank here for you to write down a dictator, president, tyrant, communist, chief, king, queen, revolutionary, that really did any good for the poor. You might have to think hard. If you leave this blank, blank, I can understand:

____

____

____

There are several Presidents of the United States, although stiffly opposed by big business that helped the poor. Can you name them?

____

____

____

Did you know Republicans fought tooth and nail against Social Security? YES...NO...

Did you know Republicans still fight tooth and nail against Social Security and want to privatize it: YES...NO...which means if they get their way while you are working you and your employer can send in a check of your own money to a private company and when you reach retirement age the private company will send you a monthly check consisting of a portion of your own money minus 10 or 15 percent for a handling fee. Would you like this? YES...NO...

Did you know that the average person only draws Social Security for several years before they die? YES...NO...What happens to all that extra money?

____

____

____

Did you know that an illegal working in the United pays into Social Security but can never draw it? YES...NO...What happens to all that extra money?

____

____

____

What happens to the money when a person who has paid into Social Security dies before he can draw any benefits?

____

____

____

How many senators and people in congress that are over 65 do you think are drawing Social Security? Circle your answer: 2 – 10 – 15 – 37 – 78 – 147 – 234 – all of the thieving bastards (even if they are not true bastards they are still bastards.) And a blank for your answer if you do not agree with any of my numbers:

____

____

____

Vent returned with a pitcher of beer and chilled glasses. Before sitting down he poured two beers with the professionalism of a good beer pourer – good head and all that. He then sat, picked up his glass, I picked up mine, and we drank. I must say that a beer that someone else has purchased really does have better flavor. Is the statement true or only in my head? YES...NO... ONLY IN MY HEAD...

"Do you want to know what the first thing was that really pissed me off and started me venting?" Vent asked.

I didn't really know if I wanted to know or not, but I answered, "Yes."

"The news on TV," Vent hollered so loud I jumped and spilt beer on my shirt, which used to bother my wife, but since she divorced me it does not bother me at all.

"What about the news?" I asked. I have always been a person who likes the news. It gives me a feeling that I really know what is going on in the world, which down deep I know is a lie, as what is really going on the news isn't going to tell you because the government hasn't told them.

Do you think the government, by not telling you what is really going on, truly believes it is for your own good? YES...NO...

Wouldn't you think that being adults we know what is good and not good for us? YES...NO...

If the government supposedly works for us what gives them the right to withhold information from us?

____

____

____

Are our leaders supposed to work for the people or control the people? WORK FOR...CONTROL...

In truth who do the people we elect really work for? A blank for your answer:

____

____

____

Vent stood. "Now watch me, I am imitating a newscaster," Vent said with no trace of anger or ventingness, which I doubt is a word but seems to fit the situation.

"Listen closely," he added.

I listened as close as I could without moving my chair closer to him. The term 'listen closely' has always been a term I do not fully understand. Can one listen 'farther'? YES...NO...

If you have ever heard anyone say, "Now listen farther" please give me an example:

____

____

____

Vent began imitating a news announcer. "Today ladies and gentlemen twenty-four people were killed in a train accident in Spain," said in a tone like where in the hell is Spain?

"Eighteen people in Wisconsin are deathly sick from eating contaminated cheese balls," said in a tone he didn't know what the hell cheese balls are.

"A suicide bomber killed four children, six women, five donkeys and two dogs in Afghanistan," said in a tone like who really cares what happens in Afghanistan anymore except the soldiers who have had to do four and five tours in one of the cesspools of the world. I will add their extended families do care and worry deeply.

"And," here Vent smiled like a gorilla that was showing off his new set of dentures, "Roslyn Palmarode, Hollywood's newest star, is checking herself into a rehab clinic because the stress of shooting two movies in one year and making fifteen million dollars has been so intense she did not have the will power to not snort eight ounces of China White while drinking fourteen shots of strawberry flavored vodka. She has tweeted that she needs all of our prayers and hopes she can return to her career within a few months."

"The government has decided the best way to get out of the deficit is to invest in Drug Cartels, since they were stupid enough to make pot illegal," said in a tone of what was the government thinking after the fiasco of prohibition.

"Junkie Bill's latest album was released three days ago and so far has sold eight million copies. Let's all wish Junkie Bill good luck, now that the government is investing in Drug Cartels heroin prices will go sky high."

"In Maine the cod fishermen are protesting that by putting limits on their catch the government is running them out of their jobs, just because there are not many cod left doesn't seem to mean anything," said in a tone that all things come to an end.

"In Miami six black men killed two white girls, sorry, black people killing white people is not supposed to be put on the news," said in an apologetic tone because the NAACP has never heard of a black person killing a white person.

"In Chicago four black gang members killed eight black members of another gang. The killers told the press the reason they killed people of their own race was because the victims were not descendants of slaves," said in a tone of how long ago was the Civil War anyway.

"Today in Syria fifty freedom fighters were killed when they clashed with other freedom fighters. The President sternly informed Syria he might send in U.S. forces to fight another useless war that would end up costing the United States so much money that even investing in the Drug Cartels could not come close making up the deficit," said in a tone of stupid is what stupid does.

"And, the singer Justin Behop today learned how to pull up his pants and speak English." Pause for contemplate all the idiots who have made Justin Behop a multi-millionaire.

"The quarterback for the Green Bay Packers has a torn muscle in his leg and will miss Sunday's game. Better change your bets." Pause for bookies to try and find people to bet the other side of the line.

"Now ladies and gentlemen time for several commercials. I know you really want to know how to be regular, have a hard dick for you unfortunate men who have a soft one, and you ladies, in between all the mayhem in life really have to know where to find shoe sales. We'll be right back."

Vent took a deep breath and then proclaimed. "That's why news pisses me off. In between news we have to hear about actors and actresses and how to get a stiff dick or if you take this pill you will not have a heart attack but your liver will rot, your hair will fall out and your finger nails will turn black."

I do know men are concerned that when they are one hundred years old they will not be able to get a hard-on, but do you really care if an actor or actress is in rehab or if they have sold their eight million dollar home and downsized into a four million dollar cabin in the woods? YES...NO...

If you do care, why?

____

____

____

After an actor or actress becomes famous they suddenly are experts on everything to do with life. They debate war, crime, poverty, animal rights, and on and on. Am I missing something? Actors are about the most unstable people there are. And, because in all things I strive to be politically correct, should a male gay actor that in his spare time wears dresses be called an actress? YES...NO...

If your answer was NO what should he be called?

____

____

____

And, truthfully, are all our politicians merely actors or actresses: YES...NO...If you circled NO what are they? Ego maniacs or idiots are not answers?

____

____

____

"For people who could care less about Hollywood or commercials there is a TV and radio station called PBS (Public Broadcasting System) that is publicly and state-funded," I said. (Author statement: I received no money, expensive trips, or any form of compensation from PBS.)

Another good news source is BBC (British Broadcasting) they give a great world report on news. Many Brits do not like BBC but they don't like the sun so what do they know.

"There are many states that do not fund PBS," Vent said, adding, "Texas is one."

"Why?" I asked, slightly alarmed, not verbalizing that Texas has to be number one in producing the worst politicians ever. Sorry all you people from Texas but I really do believe this is true and I have lived in Texas for many years.

"You would have to ask a Texas politician," Vent replied.

If you watch the news, has it ever upset you so bad you did not eat dinner? YES...NO...

Or stop you from having your after work drink? YES...NO...

Vent sipped his beer. I looked at mine. I thought back on my original quest before I saw Vent, which was a beer and a sandwich, now it was returning to sandwich. "Are you hungry?" I asked Vent.

"Are you asking me out to eat or are we going dutch?" Vent asked.

"I'll flip you for lunch," I said.

On a first date is it proper for the man to suggest to the woman they go dutch? This is for all dates of all sexual persuasions. YES...NO...and a blank:

____

____

____

Vent finished his beer, looked at the rest of the beer in the pitcher, did not pour any into his glass, reached into his pocket and pulled out a quarter. "Heads or tails," he said.

"Let me see the quarter," I said.

He handed me the quarter. It did not have two heads or two tails. I handed it back. Question: Why is it with most business deals we always feel like we are getting cheated?

Is it because capitalism is in all truth legal crime? YES...NO...

"You call," he said, tossed the coin, and slapped it on the table.

"Heads."

It was heads. "Two out of three," Vent said.

I shook my head but out of the kindness of my heart said, "I'll pay for the beer."

Question: Would you have paid for the beer? YES...NO...

"There's a nice cheap sandwich shop down the street," Vent said with the emphasis on cheap.

Bill seemed relieved when I paid the tab like he really did not want to break my legs. As Vent and I left a few people applauded and made remarks like, "You keep after the bastards Vent, we all need you to be our advocate."

Vent nodded his head like a pro golfer after making a good shot nods to the crowd, although Vent was not as full of himself, and I doubt he is making ten million a year filming commercials for golf clubs or sports drinks.

I chuckle every time I see the golf commercial where a pro golfer states he has to go see his rheumatoid arthritis doctor – most of us can't afford to go see a general practitioner. Before this commercial did you know there was such a thing as a rheumatoid arthritis doctor? YES...NO...

It had stopped raining but the heavy damp air glued the car and bus pollution to the streets in a sheet of gray smog. As we walked Vent did not wave his arms up and down or seem agitated. Maybe the pitchers of beer had a calming effect on him. In the West if a cowboy drinks several pitchers of beer he wants to get into fight and afterwards sob about how much he loves his truck and dog. He figures his wife or girlfriend is going to leave him so it is nothing to cry over – part of being a cowboy – every trade has its drawbacks. Businessmen after several pitchers of beer puke and wish they had sipped scotch and water.

As we neared the restaurant Vent informed me the majority of people that would be eating were homeless but it was not a mission. I doubted they served oysters.

The restaurant was called NEDS and I would give it no stars. NEDS was one large room with no counter and a hall that I presumed went to the kitchen. The clientele looked like an assortment of stray dogs. Men and women dressed in wrinkled and non-matching outfits sat at card tables with folding chairs. No makeup for the women, un-shaved faces for the men, and missing teeth for both seemed to be in fashion. Many had glass jars or tin cans in front of them and were counting the dimes and quarters and occasional dollar bill their panhandling had made for them during the day. For being packed NEDS was quiet as though the people felt ashamed to be sitting in a cafe and ordering food. Most of the people said hello to Vent and nodded at me. For some reason I felt embarrassed seeing the people. Why I do not know? When you walk by a homeless or poor person do you feel embarrassed? YES...NO...

If you answered YES the next question is why?

____

____

____

If you answer NO the question is also why?

___

___

___

There were posters on the grease stained off white walls for the closest AA meeting, directions to the downtown shelters, food distribution centers, where the methadone clinic was, and how to dispose of needles. There was a bus schedule. There were also signs for several churches proclaiming how God loves every one.

Here is a question for all deeply religious people. Is there room in Heaven for homeless people? YES…NO…

We sat at a corner table. The waitress was no more than nineteen or twenty. All the men in NEDS looked at her like she was the best thing in life since Pea Soup. By her perfect teeth, nice shoes, silk blouse, and pleated slacks I gathered she lived in the suburbs and only worked at NEDS to further her horizons and find out how the other half lived. When she was older she could proclaim she had been around, "Those poor dreadful people that life has abandoned." On the other hand she might feel a great empathy for the poor and realize that no matter what the city fathers say, they really could care less about the poor and homeless – they don't vote or have enough money to donate to a campaign fund – two to three thousand dollars a plate dinners have a way of limiting the voting pool. I think, but do not know for sure, that most Republicans want to cut food stamps, and make our streets look like the streets of Mexico or other South American Countries. Streets lined with beggars have a certain charm to them. Poor fuckers should have gone to Harvard – no tax paying bastards, how can we give them a break when we are giving all the tax breaks to multi-national corporations that are taking all their jobs overseas? Here is a blank for you to write a thank you note to all the large corporations that have taken the majority of their jobs overseas: You may skip this blank if you are a CEO:

____

____

____

If we declared war on homelessness could we win? YES...NO...

Why do we have homeless Veterans?

____

____

____

The waitress smiled happily at Vent. "I haven't seen you in a few weeks," she said.

"Sally, you give me the bill for all the people in here," Vent said.

"Eat up folks, the bill is on Vent," Sally announced.

"That's nice of you," I said more than a little surprised.

Vent ignored me.

The people waved at Vent with grateful smiles on their faces. Vent did not look around the room to garner praise. He was busy reading the menu which did not take a Master's in English to read as there were only six items and, since Sally knew his name, I figured he had read it before.

The menu read: Hamburger, Cheeseburger, French Fries (which we all know has nothing to do with the French) Curly Fries, Potato Chips, and Onion Rings. There were two choices for drinks – coffee or Coke – with a disclaimer that they did not mind Pepsi but they really didn't want it in their food establishment. The hamburger was $2.00, the cheeseburger $2.50 with no choice of cheese – only American. The hamburgers came with lettuce and pickles. I figured the hamburgers were about the size of a dime. There was an off brand ketchup and mustard on the table, a salt shaker but no pepper, a glass holding plastic forks, spoons, and knives, and one of those metal napkin holders that were in bus stops during WWII and are coming back in vogue in fancy diners.

"I'll have a cheeseburger and a coke," I told Sally.

"Me too," Vent said.

As Sally walked away two policemen entered NEDS. They stood at the door with scowls on their faces and scanned the room like what they were seeing was a book on the banned book list. All the men and women looked away from them in fright. I imagine they had all spent a few nights in jail for vagrancy, sleeping on street corners, drunk in public or drug possession. There was no way in hell they ran or worked for any crime organization.

Vent looked at the two cops and sprang to his feet like a chicken headed for the hen house that had spotted a hawk. The blood vessels in his neck stood out so far I thought they might burst. "What are you doing here?" he hollered pointing at the cops. "There are no crimes going on. We did not call you."

The inside of NEDS was quieter than a nun sneaking out of the convent to go play poker and not bingo. The cops glared at Vent. Vent glared back. The two cops looked at each other. "I know you didn't come in here to eat," Vent said.

One of the cops that would have made a Gestapo agent look like a Boy Scout snarled at Vent, "Don't press your luck buddy."

"I have no luck," Vent replied curtly. "But, unlike most of these unfortunate people I know my rights."

The cop looked at his cohort in a questioning manner, looked back at Vent in a 'wait till I catch you alone manner' and then they left. Every patron glanced at Vent like he was either the bravest man they had ever seen or the stupidest, which in many cases is the same thing.

Vent sat down. "I hate cops," he said but not angrily, adding, "I know they have a function, and I know they are needed, and I know there are many good ones, but the true concept of them I hate. Power over people corrupts."

Sally brought the cokes which were in the largest plastic glasses I have ever seen. She handed each of us a straw. I was impressed. Impressed or not I asked Vent, "Why do you hate cops?"

"They are puppets that only do what they are told," he said, "and the bottom line is that if the government suddenly made ashtrays illegal they would be more than happy to lock everybody up that owned an ashtray."

"I never thought about that," I said.

"You'd better start thinking," he warned.

If there was a law that ashtrays were illegal would cops arrest people who have ashtrays? YES...NO...

If ashtrays were suddenly illegal and you were out of work and did not have any money would you sell ashtrays if you could get your hands on them? YES...NO...

"Also," Vent said, "Cops are now trained like military units. It is not their job to protect the people they supposedly serve. It is their job to uphold the law. In doing this they use unethical tricks to get around laws. If a cop wants to search your car all he has to say is, I thought I smelled marijuana. Cops can shoot you and say, "It looked like he was going for a weapon" or, "I was afraid for my life."

Question: What should be done with cops that overstep their authority? Here is a list of examples:

Example: "He had a two inch pocket knife and that is why I shot him seven times in the head."

Example: "There was one of them and only six of us and that is why we beat him half to death with our night sticks."

Example: "When I shot him five times I thought I had pulled out my stun gun."

A blank for your reply as to what should be done with cops that overstep their authority?

____

____

____

Did you know that most cops that break the law do not go to jail but are merely fired? YES...NO...

"If you don't break the law you don't get in trouble," I said to Vent.

"Who writes the laws?" Vent asked.

"The ones in power," I replied and then cringed.

"You had better check into some of the new laws," Vent said in a paranoid tone.

For your information: There are 27,000 federal laws with more being added everyday. This does not count the number of state laws. It is estimated that the average person has committed six felonies and does not even know it.

Did you know it is illegal to sing Happy Birthday in a public place? YES...NO...

If you do not believe me look it up under copyrights.

Here is a word to the wise for all you people who believe in the justice system never, never, talk to the police if you are arrested – always say you want an attorney.

Here is a blank for you to fill in all the laws that have been written over the past twenty years that have eroded your rights. That is if you know any of them, which you would do well to learn: I'll start: No knock search warrants and forfeiture laws:

If you don't know the law and the cops kick in your door you have no right to cry or bitch, you might look up the phone number for the Civil Liberties Group in your area and see if they will take your case for you. If not, with our legal system the way it is, you had better have at least ten thousands dollars for an attorney. If you don't you will be assigned a public defender that normally could care less if you go to jail or not and will plead your case out. Also, you will need a carpenter to repair the door, and it will take you two or three days to clean up your house after the cops have trashed it – that alone will cost you about a thousand bucks.

There are over 20,000 no knock police raids in the United States every year. This is where the cops kick in a door and storm in with guns drawn without having to serve a warrant. In 2014 over thirty people were killed in no knock raids where nothing illegal was found. This includes several children. In Texas a man killed two cops after they kicked in his door and beat the murder charge. Who is to say somebody kicking in your door with no warning and dressed like a cop is a cop. Police are exempt from prosecution for conducting an illegal no knock raid even if a person gets killed. They are not exempt from a civil case. Go figure.

For all you people that are always relying on the Constitution to uphold your rights, are no knock searches against the Constitution? YES...NO...

Are illegal search and seizure laws against the Constitution? YES...NO...

Do you think no knock police raids should be illegal? YES...NO...

What would you do if an informant gave police wrong information and they kicked in your door, trashed your house, and tossed a stun grenade in your baby's crib?

I doubt you would say. "I understand guys, you just made a mistake."

It happened in Texas and nothing happened to the police even though the child was critically injured.

Did you know that if evidence is seized illegally it can still be used in court if the Officer states he did not know that what he was doing was illegal? YES...NO...

If I rob a store and try and tell the Judge I did not know it was illegal what would the Judge do? LAUGH...CRY...GIVE ME AN EXTRA YEAR FOR BEING STUPID.

The law states ignorance of the law is no excuse. Why is it an excuse for cops?

Are cops stupid if they do not know the law? YES...NO...

How can you uphold the law if you do not know the law? There is only one answer. You may circle it if you wish: YOU CAN'T.

"Years ago I saw a bumper sticker that said, 'next time you need a cop call a hippie,'" I said to Vent.

Vent half smiled, "Murder, rape, robbery, extortion, child molestation, assault, arson, speeding, counterfeiting, kidnapping, things of that nature are crimes, the rest of what happens in life is none of their business. What you put in your body, who you sleep with, what you eat, is none of the government's business."

Here is a blank for you to write down what you think is the government's business.

Border Patrol Agents, FBI, CIA, Sheriffs, and other law enforcement agencies are dismissed from this question. Do you like Police Officers? YES...NO...

Has the image of the police changed in the last ten years from one of trust to one of apprehension? YES...NO...Why?

Of all police officers what percentage do you think are crooked? Circle your answer: 5%, 10%, 15%, 20%, 30%, 40%, 50%. A blank for your guess:

Sally brought the two cheeseburgers. They were not the size of dimes. They were the size of a small pie plate with enough French Fries to fill two or three dozen French people's mouths and keep them from saying weird shit like, "American go home," or, "French wine is better than American wine," which even a beer drinker knows is a crock. Ask the French where all the wine starts came from after a disease wiped out their vineyards. The answer boys and girls is not Finland or Russia. To give you a hint it is a country that likes more than one or two pieces of asparagus on their plate and a portion of meat, lamb, or fish that is bigger than your toenail. Par La Vous and all that I love Paris rot. Here is a blank to explain to me why people love Paris when crime is rampant, most of the streets are filthy, it is terribly expensive, and people are about as friendly as hornets:

____

____

____

Vent and I did not talk as we ate. NEDS is not a place where polite conversation during a meal is necessary. When we finished, neither of us could eat all the fries, but two people sitting at the card table next to us eyed them like they were gold so we handed them the plates. NEDS is also not a place where it is rude to share food. In a nicer place they would have just thrown the food away. If you would like to make a comment on why we thrown away good food here are a few blanks - homeless shelters representatives, shelters for abused women representatives, and any and all of you that are sleeping on the street are extremely welcome to comment:

____

____

____

The first time I experienced real poverty was in Vietnam. I was put on garbage detail with several other guys who were as happy as I was to smell like garbage and not go out on an operation and get shot at. We drove to each unit in a deuce and a half truck and picked up 55 gallon drums filled with garbage. The dump was in a so called safe zone, and for some reason the dump had a tall fence built around it much like a prison. At the time I saw no reason for garbage to be locked up, but now that America has the highest incarcerated population in the world, even out shining China, I figure the United States was in training. The gate was manned by two MP's. Outside the fence were over one hundred ragged and bone thin children looking pleadingly into the dump. Being dutiful soldiers we showed the MP's our dump pass, drove in, and started dumping the garbage off the back of the truck. As we did children scrambled over the wire like monkeys and frantically scrounged for morsels of food. The MP's ran at them and chased them back over the wire. One of the MP's caught a child and slapped him a few times, making his nose bleed, and then tossed him over the fence like a skinny football. The guys and I looked at the MP like what we saw was not real – at the time I thought American soldiers did not hurt civilians. The MP caught and hit another child and without thinking we all jumped out of the truck and proceeded to beat the living shit out of the MP, much to the delight of the children, and only stopping when his buddy drew his 45 pistol on us. For our transgression we were never allowed to dump the garbage again and busted down a rank. I swore if I ever saw the MP again in my life I would do my best to rip his nose from his face. Thank what ever demon causes war I have never seen him as my vow still holds true to this day.

Later in life I was disillusioned by the fact that American soldiers did in fact kill many civilians (on purpose not unintentionally.)

Sally walked over. "Give me the bill would you please?" Vent said pleasantly, adding, "And the next twenty people that come in buy them a hamburger and a drink on me."

Sally went to the back and came back with a bill. Vent looked at the bill, which I figured was close to two hundred dollars, he reached into his suit inner pocket, pulled out a wad of cash a Mafia don would have been impressed by and handed Sally three one hundred dollar bills. "If there is any left it is for you," he said.

"I work for free," Sally replied. "I'll give it to someone."

I felt lower than a snail for my first thoughts about Sally. Someone should put out a trail of salt for me to sliver through.

I was also slightly taken back by the wad of cash Vent had and for a few moments I was tempted to ask, "What do you do?" Meaning: where do you work?

For a reason beyond my comprehension I have always hated the question, but I suppose where we work is really what we are whether we like it or not. I have always felt the question should be, "What are your dreams?" not "What do you do?"

"I work at Wendy's," said with a sad smile.

"I work for the city," said resolutely.

"I am a banker," said with pride.

But what are your dreams?

Question: How many people are able to make work their dream? Circle your answer: Half of mankind? A third? Ten percent? A few? A blank for the number you think is right:

____

____

____

If we all were brave enough and lucky enough to do what we wanted, or follow our dreams, would the world be a better place? YES...NO...MAYBE?

Are you doing what makes you happy? YES...NO...

I followed Vent out of NEDS in a wake of thankful nods and smiles. Here is a blank for people to write down the last time they caused people to nod and smile at them – exact times and dates are not necessary, merely the occasion. If you can't write anything down you have my sympathy:

____

____

____

It would be dark soon and the street lights were beginning to come on. Needing to be reminded that I was in the process of dying I glanced at my watch. I had first seen Samuel L. Ruthorford at 5:30. It was now 7:30. Time flies when one is drinking beer and eating hamburgers, not counting a RESTROOM break, and spirited conversation.

The traffic had thinned out and there were only a few people walking. The majority of humanity was home in the suburbs recovering from the day's work and building up strength for another. For a moment I felt stuck up in-between. I didn't want to rent a hotel room. I didn't want to drink more beer. "There's a coffee shop a few blocks away. Would you like to get a cup of coffee?" Vent asked in a way that I sensed he was concerned about me and understood my feelings. How can a person that is peeved off most of the time be concerned? If you can explain this to me here is a blank:

____

____

____

Or, on the other hand, is the reason he is peeved off most of the time because he is concerned? YES...NO...

When you are peeved off do you want to break things and act like an idiot? BREAK THINGS...ACT LIKE AN IDIOT...

Is BREAKING THINGS or ACTING LIKE AN IDIOT what you want to teach your children if you do have children? YES...NO...

For some reason the buildings reminded me of a Hitchcock movie but I couldn't remember which one. The coffee shop was not one of those fancy chain coffee shops where the employees wear the same shirt and the customers sit around with laptops discussing lattes and cappuccinos while showing off their new jogging or bicycle riding outfits. On the window, painted in white letters, was simply the word **COFFEE**. The inside was the size of a good-sized living room. The walls were dark gray and covered with posters for bands, poetry readings, a protest against Wall Street, and other things that are considered counter culture. Have you ever noticed how counter culture topics change with each generation? My generation was Vietnam. I find it strange but during the Iraq and Afghanistan Wars there were no protesters. I figure if the United States had reinstated the draft there would have been huge protests. Do you think if the United States reinstated the draft people would protest our useless wars? YES...NO...

Do you think the reason people do not chastise our soldiers now is because the country feels guilty about how they treated the Vietnam Vets? YES...NO...

The tables and chairs inside the coffee shop looked like they had been salvaged from dumpsters and were so close together they reminded me of wooden sardines. The counter was in the corner with an espresso machine and three coffee pots. The background music was low, deep and dark, and sounded like a female Leonard Cohen with a cold. The young lady behind the counter was wearing a black T-shirt. Her arms and neck were covered with brightly colored tattoos of snakes, spiders, and other crawly things. She had a silver tongue stud, a silver stud in her nose, and numerous loops hanging from her ear lobes. Her hair was red and streaked with green and she was reading a copy of Smithsonian.

I remembered the stares and hate filled glares hippies got from mainstream America. Since then I have never cared how people dress, whether their hair is long, short, green, purple or orange. I figure we are all in this life mess together and whatever it takes to get you through is fine with me. Question: Do people have to dress like you to be considered people? YES...NO. Here is a blank to explain your answer:

____

____

____

Here is a question for old hippies. Did you ever think people could look worse than we did? YES....NO...

If you answered YES, who?

____

____

____

Seeing Vent, a smile erupted on the young lady's face that was so contagious I smiled. "Vent," she said, "I haven't seen you in a few days. I was worried."

Vent returned her smile and whispered to me. "It's nice to have someone in your life that worries about you and wishes you the best."

The statement saddened me for a moment. I don't know if there is anyone in my life that worries about me.

Question: How many people do you know that worry about you? If your answer is more than one you are a very fortunate person and I am happy for you and also jealous: Circle your answer: 1 person...2 people...6 people... 12 people: A blank if there is more __________________.

We made our way to the counter. There were two couples and a lone man at other tables. Each had no shortage of tattoos and studs. The couples smiled at us and the lone man nodded. The couples went back to talking in hushed tones and the single man went back to his book. There was a black Labrador retriever sleeping on an army blanket in the corner. I was surprised he didn't have silver earrings although he might have a tongue stud but I couldn't tell as his mouth was closed.

"I would like the usual, Patricia," Vent said.

"What different types of coffee do you have?" I asked.

"We have espresso, single, double, or triple shot and black coffee, no decaffeinated. We have organic brown sugar, real milk, but no non-dairy creamer," Patricia said with a sly smile.

"I'll be," I said. "No frothy coffee drinks."

"This is a true coffee shop," Patricia stated sternly. "If you want any of that frothed up crap other coffee shops call coffee you can get your ass out of here."

"I'll take a cup of black coffee," I said liking her attitude.

Patricia's smiled slyly again. "You can buy a cup of black coffee but you cannot take one," she said.

"I will buy a cup of black coffee," I said realizing my choice of words had been truly inappropriate.

"I'll bring you your orders," she said.

We sat by the window and I noticed there was no case for pastries or sandwiches, no stand with those little high energy bars that cost five bucks, no snacks or food of any kind.

Vent knew what I was thinking. "This is a coffee shop, not a cafeteria," he said like a cafeteria was a dirty word.

Why snacks in a coffee shop are a bad thing to Vent I have no idea.

When I was a kid I was not allowed to drink coffee. Coffee was an adult thing like gin and rum and cigarettes. I didn't drink coffee religiously until I was in the army. Army coffee was black and bitter. People who put milk or sugar in their coffee were considered sissies. I apologize to anyone who puts milk or sugar in their coffee but I am only stating a point of history.

Now that most people drink flavored coffees, frothed coffees, blended coffees, and on and on, are most of us sissies? YES...NO...a blank for your reasoning:

____

____

____

Truthfully, now that I am older and wiser, I really don't care what you put in your coffee or whether you are a sissy or not. If I put anything in coffee it is Kailua or dark rum.

Patricia brought Vent a triple espresso in a real triple espresso cup, a salt sconce filled with sugar, and a tiny spoon. My cup of black coffee cup was the size of a softball and smelled like burnt toast with a dab of dirt tossed in. Vent handed Patricia a twenty dollar bill stating, "Keep the change."

"You are such a nice person," Patricia replied.

"Don't let it go to your head," Vent said.

Patricia went back to her Smithsonian Magazine and I had a feeling Vent was a good guy that only used his anger to cover the fact he was lonely. Question: Do a lot of angry people just need a hug and don't know how to ask for one? YES...NO...If you were angry and lonely would you ask a friend for a hug? YES...NO...If your answer was NO then why not?

____

____

____

I wondered once again how Vent had so much money.

"Patricia is in grad school," Vent said. "She is studying to be a molecular biologist."

I didn't know what to say so I sipped my coffee. If I drank the whole cup I would not need a plane to get back to Phoenix as I could outrun the fastest plane. I liked the coffee. It was bitter. It was real coffee. Its only function was to keep one awake. Coffee like it is supposed to be, the first Dexedrine, the first Black Beauty, the first Crank. Life would be so much better if we only drank coffee to jack ourselves up. I do know one thing. Drinking too much coffee will not get you tossed in jail for two or ten or twenty years, make your teeth fall out, or make it necessary to rob a grocery store so you can afford your fix.

Vent put a tiny spoonful of sugar in his coffee, stirred it a few times, then shot his triple shot of espresso down like it was a dram of whiskey. He made a face like he was sucking on a persimmon and sighed deeply.

I have never sighed after drinking coffee. I have burped, choked, burnt my lips, grimaced, but I have never sighed. But, who am I? Have you ever sighed after drinking coffee? YES...NO... If your answer was YES please explain why.

____

____

____

Here is a blank for you to list drinks, both with alcohol and not, that have made you sigh. Once again I have never had a drink that makes me sigh. I have had drinks that made me puke and gave me a headache.

____

____

____

If you would, please send me a copy of the drinks you have listed as I will try them. Sighing in life is not a bad thing. It releases a lot of stress and built up anger. Which, I must admit, I am full of.

Are you full of anger and stress like I am? YES...NO...

If your answer is YES then you should be smarter than me and stop doing what you are doing and do something else.

If your answer was NO you are a fortunate person.

After the espresso blasted through Vent's veins his eyes narrowed to slits and his gaze seemed to penetrate my brain. He leaned forward like he was the bad cop in the bad cop good cop routine who was interrogating a guy for not putting enough quarters in a parking meter and said in a demanding tone, "Well William, tell me what you think about abortion?"

I sipped my coffee, placed the cup down, picked the cup up again and took another sip, set the cup down, and then scratched my chin. "Answer me!!" Vent hollered loud enough the dog sleeping in the corner opened his eyes, raised his head slowly, looked over at us inquisitively, then decided what ever all the noise was about was not worth the time to get up and bark and went back to sleep.

Patricia, the two couples, and the single man did not bother to look over. Vent's reputation preceded him.

"I think it is a woman's right to choose," I said but with little conviction.

"Exactly," Vent bellowed and slammed his fist down on the table. "It is not the government's business. It is not any religion's business. It's not anyone's business but the woman."

"It's sad, though," I said.

Vent slumped in his chair and the fire went out of his eyes. "Any woman who has had an abortion will never forget it," he said barely above a whisper.

Do you think abortion is a happy thing? YES...NO...

Do you think a woman has the right to make her own decisions? YES...NO...

Why are most children in orphanages not adopted?

____

____

____

You would think all the deeply religious people that have so much time to protest outside of abortion clinics would have enough money to adopt all the children in orphanages.

Why do people and governments like to get into other people's business?

____

____

____

And to muddle the issue what do you think about the morning after pill? Is it an abortion? YES...NO…

____

____

____

If you do not believe in abortion what about a woman that has been raped and becomes pregnant, do you think it was God's will? YES...NO...

If you answered YES what kind of God would sanction rape?

____

____

____

Vent waved at Patricia and within thirty seconds Patricia brought Vent a double espresso, looked to see that he still had sugar and noticed my cup was still three fourths full. "You don't like my coffee?" Patricia asked in a slightly offended tone.

"It's the best coffee I've had in years," I replied telling a white lie. It was good, but it was not the best. The best coffee I ever drank was in a corner stand by the pier in Bremerton, Washington. Don't get me wrong though, it didn't make me sigh. It might have been the fact it was 38 degrees, raining, and I was shivering so bad I looked like a heroin addict that had been sold a gram of instant cocoa.

Patricia half smiled at me letting me know she knew I was telling a white lie.

Question: Are white lies good or bad things? GOOD...BAD...and a blank to explain your answer. Don't tell me that you have never told one.

____

____

____

Vent put the same amount of sugar in his cup he had used for his triple espresso. I took another sip of my coffee, feeling the need to finish it or disappoint Patricia.

I couldn't take it anymore, and even though I knew Vent might not like me invading his privacy, I had to ask. "Vent, what do you do to have so much money?" Admit it, we are all nosey. There is no need to even ask YES or NO if we are nosey.

Vent shot his double espresso, looked at me as calmly as a man who has consumed five shots of espresso can, and said, "My father was a truck driver and my mother was a waitress. We were borderline poor but we always ate. Mom and Dad grew a large garden in the backyard and my Dad hunted and fished. I mowed yards and did odd jobs around the neighborhood. My parents always implored me to save my money. As a kid I saved half of every dollar I made. During the army I saved 90% of my check. Many years ago I read an article about an upstart company and I invested nine thousand of the ten thousand dollars I had."

"What was the company you invested in?" I asked.

"A little company called Microsoft," Vent said like it was no big deal. "I have made millions."

The statement shocked me and it made no sense. Vent did not look rich. His clothes would have been cheap at a thrift shop. He was not wearing a gold watch, a gold bracelet, or a diamond pinky ring. He was not driving a fancy car.

"I live in a two bedroom apartment not far from here," Vent said. "I don't own a car. I don't peddle a bicycle. I give 60% of my money to various charities. I don't need it."

"Are you a Buddhist?" I asked.

Vent laughed sarcastically. "No, I don't believe in owning a bunch of stuff," he said.

"If I had money I would own a bunch of stuff," I had to admit.

"Why?" Vent asked and gave me a look like if I answered the question wrong he would vent all over my head and shoulders with his fists.

There had to be a good answer but what ever the answer was, was not inching its way from my brain to my lips. It is a fact brains and lips can get into a lot of trouble together. "Answer me," Vent asked but did not demand.

"I really don't know," I replied, but then several answers came to me that I did not verbalize.

I wanted to be better than anyone else.

I wanted everyone to know I was rich, and to repeat myself, let them know I was better than they were. I need six cars, four houses, an island, a jet, three boats, eighty-two pairs of shoes, nine closets filled with clothes, race horses, diamonds, rubies, paintings, a yard staff, maids, all to make me feel I am worthy.

Does a person having money and possessions make them better than the majority of people? YES...NO...

Although it is too late to catch Microsoft on the upswing, here is a line to state what you would do if you had more money than you knew what to do with:

____

____

____

I knew a guy in my failed college career that became a big coke dealer (not the kind that comes in a bottle and has too much sugar) and made millions of dollars. When they caught him his excuse was he wanted to buy Brazil. He is now half way through a thirty-five year vacation at one of our finer federal correctional institutes. The only things he is trying to buy are sandwiches from the guard's kitchen. He found out the hard way it is difficult to buy a Federal Judge. Now a State Judge might be a different story - especially if the Judge is from the southern part of the United States, not to forget Chicago.

Question: Why are the South and Chicago so famous for corrupt judges?

____

____

____

For your information, it is hard to buy a Federal Judge because they make a lot of money and have a great retirement.

The guy doing time now has a Master's Degree in Business and is working on a Doctorate in Deviant Behavior, paid by you, that is if you pay taxes. When he gets out he is going to open an expensive rehabilitation drug and alcohol clinic for rock stars, actors, and politicians, teaching them at the same time how to clean all their illicit money in offshore shell corporations.

Vent, with the full effect of five shots of espresso running through his veins, started twitching around in his chair like a little kid that had to pee. For no apparent reason I asked Vent, "What do you thinking about spying on countries that are our friends and allies?"

"Every country spies on every country William," he said to me like I had to be as naive as a sixteen-year-old girl that had fallen in love with a rock star and thought he would leave his internationally known model girlfriend for her.

"But why?" I asked.

"Because throughout history allies seem to have a way of becoming enemies," Vent replied adding, "Genghis Kahn summed it up when he said an enemy of my enemy is my friend."

"Do you mean a country cannot trust another country even though they say they are friends?" I asked.

"Think about this," Vent said. "At one time England was our enemy. At one time France was an enemy of England. Germany was an ally with Russian and England. Japan was once our enemy and China our ally. Russia was our ally and now is our Enemy. We invaded Mexico. We invaded Hawaii. At one time every country in Europe has fought a war against each other. Need I go on?"

Since my knowledge of world history is lacking I saw no need for Vent to go on but I got his point.

Question: Is there really such a thing as an ally that can be trusted? YES...NO...

Do you really trust those sly Brits? YES...NO...

Or how about the Pakistani's? YES...NO...

Or the leaders in Afghanistan? YES...NO...

How about Mexico? YES...NO...

I know many Mexicans don't trust Mexico or they wouldn't be streaming across the border.

Here is a blank for you to list the countries that you trust. I will start it off: Canada.

____

____

____

Here is a blank for you to write why you trust the countries you have listed:

____

____

____

Do you think our allies spy on us? YES...NO...

Have you ever spied on your neighbor? YES...NO...

How many countries do you think trust us? Circle your answer: 0...2...6....21... 74...or a blank for your guess _____ and a long blank for you to list your answers:

____

____

____

And a question with only one answer. If you have children have you ever spied on your children? YES...

Does it make you feel guilty? YES...NO...

Do you really think that the United States only recently started spying on its own citizens? YES...NO...

If you do, you had better read up on Hoover. Hoover the FBI guy not the vacuum cleaner.

Did you know that the police now have a camera that can look through the walls of your house and have been using the device without a warrant? YES...NO...

Is this against your Constitutional rights? YES...NO...

In the modern world I can find out everything I want to know about you in close to an hour: Your age, phone number, parents, siblings, work history, military history, criminal history, credit history, where you live, need I go on. Edward Snowden did not release any classified information about NSA spying on us that down deep we really didn't suspect – maybe we merely wanted to ignore it like we ignore poverty in our own country.

For your information there are laws that govern how the government can gather information about you, but these laws do not govern what corporations or information brokers can do. If you want to scare yourself it is worth a few hours of your time to investigate this matter. Do corporations gather information legally on people and then sell it to the government?

YES...NO...If you circled NO I hate to tell you, you are wrong.

The most famous and diabolical spying incident in recent time was The New England Patriots football team spying on other football teams. Can you imagine? Knowing this do you trust their coach? YES...NO...

Or is it the truth that cheaters win and no one really cares? YES...NO...

A black man entered the coffee shop. I suppose I should say a man of color entered the coffee shop but I have a problem with that - the problem being all people are a color. If I remember correctly white is a color. Yellow is a color. Brown is a color. Off brown is a color. Red is a color. So if anyone is offended because I stated a black man walked into the coffee shop I don't know what to tell you. You can call me a white person anytime you want and I won't get offended. If there is a white person reading this that is offended by being called white here is a blank for you to explain why:

____

____

____

If there is a person of any color that is offended by being labeled by the color of their skin here is a blank for you to explain why:

____

____

____

If there are any Native Americans reading this book are you truly offended by the Washington Redskins football team's name? YES...NO...and why?

____

Do you think Dolphins and Broncos are upset at the Miami and Denver football teams? YES...NO...

How about the Detroit Redwings hockey team? Do they have blackbirds all over the country up in arms? YES...NO...

A serious question: Have we taken this race thing a little too far? YES...NO...

A blank for your reasoning:

Here is a list of questions:

Have you ever made a racist statement? If you are truthful I think there is only one answer: YES...NO...

If you have made a racist statement was it because you were angry or do you really hate people that are a different color than you? YES...NO...

Did you feel bad after you made the statement? YES...NO...

Did it make you feel better? YES...NO...

Did it make you feel superior? YES...NO...

Is god damn a racist statement? YES...NO...

For your information: More black people kill black people than whites kill blacks in the United States. More white people kill white people than blacks kill whites in the

United States. This is true for all races living in the United States. Did you know this? YES...NO...

Do you know why the above statement is true? YES...NO...I will tell you and I bet if you circled YES you will find out your reasoning is wrong. More black people kill black people because black gangs kill other black gangs. More white people kill each other because the white criminal element kills other white criminal elements. Italian gangsters kill other Italian gangsters. Irish crooks kill Irish crooks. Chinese gangs kill other Chinese gangs. Vietnamese gang members kill other Vietnamese gang members. Mexican gangs kill Mexican gangs. Biker gangs kill other biker gangs. Colombian gangs kill Colombian gangs. Here is a blank for you to list other gangs that kill each other.

____

____

____

I will guarantee you a white gang in Chicago is smart enough to keep out of a black gang's territory. And, unless you are in a Chinese gang you had better keep out of illegal dealings in any Chinatown in the world.

Merely for information one of the strongest gangs in the country now are the Russians. They control a huge part of the illegal gas operations and are almost impossible for the FBI to infiltrate.

It is also true that white cops kill more black offenders and black cops kill fewer offenders of any color. Is this because black police officers have more empathy? YES...NO...

If your answer was YES... Why?

____

____

____

If your answer was NO... Why?

____

____

____

To get back to the story: A black man walked into the coffee shop. He was wearing blue sweats and running shoes. His head was shaved and he was built like Atlas. Seeing Vent he headed for our table with a smile on his face like he had run into a friend he had not seen in years. "Good to see you Vent," the man said, pulling a chair up to the table and sitting.

"I see you are still jogging," Vent said like jogging was a four letter word when in fact it is a seven letter word, but then he smiled and shook hands with the man.

"I would like you to meet a friend of mine," Vent said to me. "William this is Sam Jones. We had the misfortune of being in the army together."

Sam and I shook hands, with me thinking it was nice to be introduced and not ignored. I have been with people that when other people joined us I was not introduced. It always upsets me and makes me wonder if I am an alien or forgot to use deodorant. Here is a question: Do you feel like you have not put on deodorant if you are not introduced. YES...NO...

Are we social creatures? YES...NO...

If we are social creatures why are there so many incidences in life when we are ignored?

____

____

____

"I haven't seen you in awhile," Sam said to Vent.

"I have started working on a new novel," Vent replied.

It had completely slipped my mind that Bill the bartender had told me Vent was a writer.

"What is it about?" Sam asked which is the normal question a writer is asked.

"It's about people that ask too many questions?" Vent said in a tone that both Sam and I knew there was no way either one of us was going to find out what the novel was about and truthfully is was none of our business.

Patricia brought Sam a cup of coffee. I gathered Sam was a regular. "I'll put it on your monthly tab," she said.

No doubt Sam was a regular. I have never been a regular at any establishment, at least not regular enough to be able to run a tab for a month. My tab lasts until it is time to go. Thinking about it, it would be nice to be able to run a tab for a week or a month – there is trust in a tab. Are there any of you that are able to run a tab? Lay away, credit card debt, mortgage, car payment, etc. etc. does not count. YES...NO...and a blank for you to list the establishments that trust you enough to run a tab:

____

____

____

Vent headed for the RESTROOM. He did not announce his departure as he knew neither Sam nor I are his mother. "Vent is a strange guy," Sam said in a way that was not derogatory.

I really didn't know what to say. Yes he is strange or no he is not strange did not seem right.

"He saved my life in the army," Sam said without any great show of emotion. "I was shot in the leg and pinned down and he crawled out and dragged me back to safety."

I was amazed and also in awe. Bravery has never been one of my strong points, although I suppose when I was in the army I was brave, but truth be known, most of the time I was afraid.

"I now run a homeless shelter," Sam continued. "Whenever we really need money Vent helps us."

"Do you see each other often?" I asked.

Sam shook his head. "Only when we run into each other or I need help for the shelter. There is nothing really to talk about. He knows how I feel about him and I know how he feels about me. I also know he wants no gratitude for saving my life."

Question: Do we all seek gratitude when we do a good or brave deed? YES...NO...

If we do seek gratitude does it diminish the deed? YES...NO...and a blank for your reasoning:

____

____

____

If you know how deeply you feel for someone and how they feel for you do you really have to see them all the time? YES...NO...

"Has he ever let you read any of his novels?" I asked.

"So far I figure Vent has written about thirty novels, but when he finishes one he prints out a copy, puts it in a box, and stacks them in his closet. He has never let me read one and to my knowledge no one else either," Sam replied.

I have heard about closet writers - people that write and then do not try and place their work with publishers. Some people say they are paranoid and cannot take rejection, others say they are true artists and don't want to demean their art by making any money. If I was a writer I would want the recognition, plus rejection has been a major part of my life so it is no big deal, I can deal with it. If you were a writer would you try and have your work published? YES…NO… and a blank for your reasoning:

____

____

____

Could you take rejection? YES…NO…

If your answer was either YES or NO explain why:

____

____

____

I suppose the fact that Vent is rich and does not have to make any money on his writing might make a difference. But there are many modern authors and also authors from the past that made large amounts of money and never stopped writing.

"How long have you known Vent?" Sam asked.

I looked at my watch – yes, I am closer to dying. "About three hours," I answered.

"What sign are you?" Sam asked in a serious tone.

Vent rejoined us. "I was born in May," I answered.

Vent started to wave his arms up and down once again trying to defeat gravity. He bellowed at Sam. "Are you getting into that astrology bullshit again?"

"It is not bullshit," Sam replied defiantly.

Vent clutched his head in both hands and shut his eyes like he had a migraine. After a few moments he opened his eyes, let his arms fall to his side and stated calmly, "Our galaxy is moving through the universe at approximately 2.7 million miles an hour. The universe is approximately 78 billion light years across. The universe is expanding. So if you believe that the alignment of the stars and moons and all that rot has something to do with your life it is absurd. There is no true alignment because all alignments are changing constantly."

Myself I never believed the stars or planets or moons or space dust have had anything to do with how my life has bounced around like a lopsided basketball, so his statement meant nothing to me, except the fact the galaxy is traveling at 2.7 million miles an hour made me a little queasy, but I can get sea sick while taking a bath.

"What you are saying is there is no center or fixed point," Sam said, "and without a center or fixed point astrology is not valid."

"Exactly," Vent replied.

"Fuck you," Sam said, "I believe the stars and moon play an important part in our life."

"Stupid people can believe in anything," Vent said.

Do you believe in astrology? YES...NO...a blank for your reasoning:

____

____

____

Do you believe stupid people can believe in anything? YES...NO...and another blank for your reasoning:

____

____

____

Do you believe little fat guys with bald heads, creatures with sixteen arms, women with a multitude of breasts, cows, monkeys, cats, can be gods and demons? YES...NO....once again another blank:

____

____

____

Do you believe it is possible for a woman to have a baby without having sex? YES...NO...

Is it possible that people from space visited the Earth, put Mary in a trance, and artificially inseminated her? YES...NO...

Do you believe if a population is starving they should eat the cows that roam around their streets that they believe are sacred? YES....NO...

Do you believe that the reason the Cubs cannot win a pennant or have not been in the World Series since 1945 is because their moon is in retrograde and there have always been too many Pisces and Cancers on the team and not enough Taurus's? YES...NO...

For either answer please tell me why the Cubs have such rotten luck?

"What do you believe in if not astrology?" Sam asked Vent.

"I believe that people can believe in anything they want but I retain the right to believe they are stupid if they think a person's life is dictated by the position of the stars," Vent said.

Sam started to laugh, but not mockingly. Vent laughed. I didn't see anything funny so I sipped on my coffee. Sam stopped laughing, gulped his coffee down, shook hands with Vent, said to me, "Nice to meet you," and left. The last time I saw him he was jogging around the corner.

"He's a good man," Vent said after Sam was gone. "After the war he started a shelter."

I didn't inform Vent I knew.

Question: Just because you do not believe what another believes is that a good reason to not be friends? YES...NO...

Is it possible there is more than one God? YES...NO...

Is it possible God or Gods are merely messing with us? YES...NO...

Is it possible that God or Gods are women? YES...NO...

Is it possible that God or Gods are mere children and are having growing pains? YES...NO...

Is it possible that God or Gods are also seasick because the galaxy is traveling 2.7 million miles an hour through the universe? YES....NO...

Is it possible that the Roman Gods, the Greek Gods, the Druid's Gods, the Cave Man's Gods, all Gods for all people in the past were real? YES...NO...

But, even if they were not real did they serve their purpose? YES...NO...

Why does man have to believe in a God to try and be good? Why can't mankind believe in themselves and be good? This is not a YES or NO question. Here are several lines.

____

____

____

Do you believe the lines in your hands, the knots on your head, the curve of your nose, the fact you are knock-kneed, pigeon-toed, cross-eyed, buck-toothed, has anything to do with how your day is going to go? YES...NO...

I had a friend when I went through my hippie stage that believed in voodoo and the future could be foretold by a witch doctor looking at chicken guts. One day another hippie told him there had been a scientific study and it was proven frog guts worked better. My friend went off the deep end, went to college, became a doctor and converted to Catholicism. The person who told him about the frog guts ate one too many psilocybin mushrooms and is spending the rest of his life in a nut house in Denver talking to little green men that promise him when he dies he will turn into a rainbow.

I finished my coffee, checked the time, I am still dying. Did you know that you are dying slower if you live in the arctic? YES...NO...

I will let you look up the answer as to why.

Did you know that the Earth is spinning at close to 2,400 miles an hour? YES...NO...

Did you know that 96% of space is unaccounted for? YES...NO...

Why do most of us believe, that what we believe, is the only answer to the riddle of life?

____

____

____

What is the riddle to life?

____

____

____

Vent waved at Patricia. There was no way he wanted another shot of espresso. Patricia came over promptly like a good waitress should. "I would like a single shot of espresso and my friend here would like another cup of coffee," Vent said.

I cringed because my heart was already doing caffeine induced mini back flips. "Since you do not want to go to a motel you might as well stay up all night and then you can sleep on the plane," Vent said.

"When I close you can stay here if you like," Patricia said to me, well aware of the effects of caffeine and the fact that walking around downtown Kansas City late at night would be the pursuit of a death wish.

To not slight any big cities downtown section – walking around downtown in any big city at night is the pursuit of a death wish.

"Thank you," I replied to Patricia, "but I will go to the airport when Vent and I are done visiting."

Here is a blank for all big cities in the country, world, and universe, to write their name if they think their downtown is safe late at night: It is a small blank:

____

If by chance you listed New York City you are an extreme optimist and will most likely have many disappointing times in your life – one of which is getting killed downtown.

"Vent," I said. "What do you think about illegal immigration?"

Vent took a deep breath and exhaled slowly. His arms did not flap up and down. His eyes did not bug out to the size of silver dollars. He took another deep breath and exhaled slowly. I wondered if he was into some Zen breathing ritual and maybe, if the truth be known, he was really 3,000 years old. "It is complicated," he said.

Patricia brought the coffees. Merely breathing the steam I knew I would not sleep for at least a week – the hell with sleeping on the airplane. If there was no turbulence I could walk up and down the aisle and peeve off the flight attendant while she was trying to serve coffee, beer, wine, mixed drinks, soft drinks and peanuts. Here is a weird question: Remember when a flight attendant was called a stewardess? YES...NO...

How about a maintenance man was called a janitor? YES...NO...

And before a secretary was a personal assistant? YES...NO...

Here is a blank for people to list the new names for the same old jobs:

____

____

____

And a blank for people to explain why with the same old jobs with brand new fancy titles the wages have not changed:

____

____

____

Are the masses really that easy to placate? YES...NO...

Back to my original question: "Vent, what do you think about illegal immigration?"

Vent's reply, "It is complicated."

"Why?" I asked.

"I'll talk about Mexico and South America and the United States," Vent said, "although illegal immigration by Asians into Canada is epidemic and Europe is also being overrun by many races – mostly Muslims and Africans trying to get out of war zones. People try to smuggle themselves into other countries for the same reasons – they have no hope of survival where they live. What would you do if you were a Mexican or South American and so poor and destitute you had no other choice than to try to get into the United States?"

"I imagine I would try to get into the United States," I replied.

"Of course you would," Vent said. "And when you got here your options are to work on farms, clean houses, mow yards, or other menial jobs."

"Those are jobs that illegal aliens take from our own people," I said.

"Bullshit," Vent said sarcastically. "They are usury jobs that most Americans won't do. For years the government turned their heads at the pitiful conditions illegal immigrants worked and lived in. The reason they turned their heads was because the farmers, garment factories, slaughter houses, and places like them were making a lot of money from cheap labor."

"People could go through the process and get into the country legally," I said.

"Only if you have the money, plus it takes years to go through the process," Vent said. "Starving people don't have a lot of patience."

If you were Mexican or South American and starving would you try to get into the United States? YES...NO...

If you were a Mexican or South American and had money would you try to go through the legal process to become an American citizen? YES...NO...

If your answer was YES how would you become a citizen legally if you had no money?

____

____

____

Is it possible to stop illegal immigration? YES...NO... If you answer was YES here is a blank to explain how:

____

____

____

If your answer was NO here is a blank to explain why not:

____

____

____

The United States has 5,500 miles of border with Canada, 1,989 miles of border with Mexico, and 95,000 miles of shoreline. How many soldiers would it take to man the land border? 10,000...25,000...50,000...1,237,462...a blank for your estimate:

____

____

____

How many ships would it take to control our shoreline? 10...24...75...463...1,208... and a blank for your estimate:

___

___

___

For your information: There are 21,000 Border Patrol Agents. They have 260 aircraft and 300 boats.

The Coast Guard has 42,000 active members, 210 aircraft and 50 ships.

There are 360,000 active members in the National Guard.

550,000 people in the Army.

196,000 people in the Marines.

320,000 people in the Navy.

335,000 people in the Air Force.

If the countries were reversed and the poor in this country had no options and you were poor would you try to smuggle yourself into Mexico or South America even if your only hope was to pick fruit or vegetables or be a maid or gardener? YES...NO...

For the same reasons would you try and smuggle yourself into Canada? YES...NO...

Why do our biggest employers in this country go out of their way to keep wages so low anyway? A blank for your reasons:

___

___

___

Do big corporations take their jobs overseas because they care if you starve? YES...NO...

Like Vent said, "It is complicated."

"Some people want to send troops to the border and shoot illegal aliens," I said to Vent.

"It is a great country that kills women and children and people coming here for hope and a new life. Bring me your masses and your huddled poor and all that lying bull-shit," Vent said, then, without waving his arms or his eyes bulging out he added, "I think everyone is this country whose ancestors came from somewhere else in the world should have to go back to wherever they came from, excluding the blacks since they did not come here from their own free will. Then the blacks and the remaining Native Americans, which our ancestors tried their best to genocide, could start their own war to decide who would control America."

Question: Should all people whose ancestors were not born in America have to go back to where they came from, which they sure as hell didn't leave because their life was good, if it had been good you would still be in what ever country your ancestors came from? YES...NO...

"That is impossible," I said. "All of our ancestors were immigrants."

"No shit," Vent replied, giving me a look like where did all these stupid people come from.

Question: If we want to be a country that lives up to what we want the world to perceive us as being can we in all truth turn on backs on immigrants? YES...NO...

As to the question that illegal immigrants steal our jobs how many people do you know that when they are out of work become maids, gardeners, or go out into fields and pick crops? Circle your answer: 2, 5, 10, 17, 147, 0, and a space if I missed a number:

Did you know that before we entered WWII many Jewish people were denied entry into the United States? At first a bill to let 20,000 Jewish children into the country was rejected then a ship carrying close to 900 Jewish people was turned away by Cuba, Canada, and the United States. The UK, Belgium, and France finally accepted some of the people. Close to 50% were returned to Germany and died in concentration camps.

Vent drank his cup of espresso without adding sugar. I finished my coffee. I felt like my feet had wings and my heart was an over excited tom tom. If the caffeine racing through my system was a vitamin pill I would not have to take another vitamin for 2,000 years. Vent looked calm, but my grandfather used to drink black coffee before he went to bed and he slept like a rock – go figure.

Speaking about vitamin pills did you know that scientist say if you have a decent diet vitamin pills do nothing for you except make your urine darker yellow? YES...NO...

Do you agree with this? YES...NO...

"I have a question for you," Vent said. "I'm tired of answering your questions."

"But you are Vent," I said. "You are supposed to wave your arms up and down and react to the absurdities in life or at least to what you think are absurdities."

"And you are William," Vent said, which didn't make any sense to me but seemed to make a great deal of sense to Vent.

"What is your Question:" I conceded, wondering at the same time if the majority of people believe in absurd things, which would make the absurd things the norm, is there then no such thing as absurdity? YES...NO...and a blank for your absurd or not absurd answer:

____

____

____

"What do you think about gun control?" Vent asked.

I laughed. "It is not a funny question," Vent said seriously.

"It's a sarcastic laugh," I replied.

"Now answer the question," Vent said sounding like my mother when I was trying to get out of doing the dishes when I was a kid. But her tone of voice was a warning that if I didn't get to work she was going to bonk me upside my head with either her shoe or a wooden spoon. In our modern times a bonk upside the head would be called child abuse and I could sue her. But since we did not have a lot of money it wouldn't have done me any good anyway. If you remember I was raised in the military and contrary to popular belief people in the military do not make a lot of money (excluding Generals – they make a lot.) The government pays its soldiers much like corporations pay their workers. Never forget boys and girls the government is in all truth nothing more than a big business – not a very good business as they can't seem to do anything but get deeper in debt. How can the government pay lousy wages and still get deeper in debt? Here is a blank if you know how:

____

____

____

When the government is thinking about either starting or participating in some obscure war they open up the flood gates for enlistment into the military. As soon as they realize the war was a big mistake, or have made all the money they can for private companies that make billions of dollars in the War Industry, they discharge many military personal before they can get any form of retirement. Is this right? YES...NO...

WARNING!! If you are considering joining any branch of the military you should investigate completely what your VA Benefits really are, not what the recruiter tells you they are. And, talk to more than one veteran – not all veterans think their service was worth their time or sacrifice.

Back to the question concerning gun control: "People who think laws can be passed that will control who can get a gun are complete idiots," I said emphatically.

"I can't disagree," Vent replied. "But tell me why?"

"Because if guns are illegal the gun trade will become like the war on drugs or the war on booze or the war on whatever. It will fail. Organized crime will take over the gun trade."

"Another thing," Vent said. "I would hate to see a country where only cops could have guns."

Question: Do you think guns can be controlled? YES...NO...

If your answer was YES, how?

____

____

____

Do you think if guns were made illegal there would be no guns? YES...NO...

Before there were guns did governments try to make bows illegal? YES...NO...

How about swords and knives? YES...NO...

Do you think if there were no guns would man still find a way to kill each other? YES...NO...

If guns were illegal would you see a great increase in bow, crossbow, and pellet gun sales? YES...NO...

How about sling shots? YES...NO...

Blow guns with poison darts? YES...NO...

Would you like it if only cops had guns? Cops are not permitted to answer this one. YES...NO...

If you wanted to buy a gun and you did not want to go to a store and go through the state and federal checks could you buy a gun? YES...NO...

If guns were made illegal would you still keep one in your house for that not so nice guy that likes to steal people's stuff? YES...NO...

The constitution states to the understanding of many people the individual has a right to keep and bear arms. Many people believe the second amendment means only a militia has the right to bear arms. For either side of the debate does this mean I can own a tank? YES...NO...

A machine gun? YES...NO...

A grenade launcher? YES...NO...

A mortar? YES...NO...

A 105 artillery piece? YES...NO...

A flame thrower? YES...NO...

How about anti-tank mincs? YES...NO...

Or anti-personal mines to put in my front yard so dogs can't piss on my grass? YES...NO...

How about a missile with a nuclear war head? YES...NO...

Or a B-25 bomber with 1,000 pound incendiary bombs? YES...NO...

When the constitution was written rifles could only fire one bullet at a time, the same with pistols, and the cannon was the weapon of mass destruction. So, if we really follow the constitution the right to bear arms only applies to single shot weapons and cannons. Is this statement absurd? YES...NO...

Truthfully, is there a need for people to own a machine gun or a semi-automatic?" Vent asked.

"There are many guns there is no need for people to own," I replied. "I don't need a rifle with a 50 round clip to hunt deer or protect my home. I don't need a sniper rifle."

Do you need a sniper rifle? YES...NO...

Do you need a 50 round clip to kill Bambi? YES...NO...

How about a squirrel, elk, moose, bear or any other animal? YES...NO...

If you do I have to say you are one lousy shot.

"Around 300,000,000 people in the United States own guns. There are 11 guns produced every minute in the United States and there is an average of 341,000 gun thefts each year," Vent said.

"Do you own a gun?" I asked Vent.

"No," Vent replied, "and you."

"No," I answered, "and I live in a state with the most wide open gun laws in the country."

"Anyone caught with a gun doing a crime should not be sent to prison but sent to a front line unit or a covert unit. Then they will find out how bad they really are," Vent said.

Question: What do you think about sending violent criminals into covert military units instead of prison? YES...NO...

Question: What do you think of covert military units? Are they good? YES...NO...

Are they needed? YES...NO...

Should the United States send secret military units into other countries to kill people? YES...NO...

Should we assassinate leaders of countries that are into genocide, ethnic cleansing, or is it any of our business? I will even give you three options: YES...NO...MAYBE...and a blank for your explanation:

____

____

____

How many countries do you think there are that have covert military units that could harm the United States? Circle your answer: 1, 5, 6, 8, 10, 12, 16, 27, 30, 31, a blank for a number if you think none of the above numbers are correct:

____

____

____

The C.I.A. made a ton of money smuggling coke, not the kind you drink. Is this weird or just me thinking it is weird? YES...NO...

Since the CIA smuggled illegal drugs do you think they also smuggle guns to fringe groups around the world? YES...NO...If you circled NO you had better do some research.

Who do you think is supplying all the terrorist groups in the world with guns and ammunition?

____

____

____

Since the terrorists are receiving so many weapons wouldn't you think we should be able to stop the supply chain? YES...NO...

Completely out of context: When I was in the infantry I figured I might get shot. Since I volunteered for the infantry there was no reason for me to bitch about it. People in the infantry shoot people and get shot. It is understood. Why is it that when cops get shot police all over the country go into an uproar? If you joined the police force you have to know your chances of getting shot are far greater than if you decided to be a bus driver or a high school teacher, after all, you are dealing with criminals as your client base. Am I right or wrong on this issue? RIGHT...WRONG...

I am sad when cops get shot, unless he was a bad cop, but I also feel he put himself into the situation. We all make choices. Don't blame the world for your choices. Is this belief out of line: YES...NO...and a blank:

____

____

____

Here is a serious statement. When a cop kills an unarmed person there is always a wave of anti-cop sentiment that sweeps through the country. My question is why don't the people that feel like they have been offended by a bad cop go after the guilty cop? A blank for your answer:

____

____

____

There was recently a man who killed three cops because two other cops had shot an unarmed man? Why didn't the man who killed the three cops that had nothing to do with the murder not shoot the two cops who had shot the unarmed man? I don't have an answer but here is a blank if you do:

____

____

____

Why does the United States lead the world in police shootings of unarmed people? Is it because heavily armed police are afraid of unarmed people? YES…NO…

Is it because the cops just really want to kill someone that is unarmed? YES…NO…

Is it because cops are such bad shots they cannot shoot the unarmed person in the leg and not six times in the chest and face? YES…NO…

Should it be against the law for cops to shoot and kill an unarmed person? YES…NO…

If I was holding a gun and you ran at me with a stick and I shot you six times and killed your dumb ass would I be charged with murder? I'll answer this one for you. YES I would and I would go to trial.

Which leads to this question. The majority of time when a cop shoots and kills and unarmed person why are they not charged with murder?

____

____

____

And don't give me that hogwash that every unarmed person that is killed by the cops wanted to commit suicide by police.

And, why do cops carry stun guns if not to use them?

Should bad cops be sent to jail or merely released from the force like they normally are? JAIL...RELEASED...

Are cops, because they are cops, exempt from the same laws that govern us? YES...NO...

Did you know that you have the right to defend yourself from an illegal arrest even to the extent of shooting the police? YES...NO...

The statement is true but also precarious – remember cops can lie to uphold the law.

Vent looked at his empty espresso cup. I looked at my empty coffee cup which left no debate if it was half full or half empty – it was empty, except for a black stain at the bottom of the cup. The question of half full or half empty never meant a thing to me. Who really cares? The question is – are you going to drink what is ever in the container or not or sit there and debate whether it is half full or half empty? Which makes me want to ask this Question: Why is it that the majority of the people a person talks to always try to sound like a philosopher? For example: You want to make small talk – stay away from war, religion, on and on so you say to a person,

"It's warm today."

The person you are talking to says, "It is always warm this time of year. It is supposed to be warm."

What is wrong with a simple, YES it is warm, or NO it is not warm.

Another example, you say to a person, "I like that red car."

The person replies, "Red is the color of aggression and the colors of cars that are in vogue reflect the mood of the country."

I mean what the fuck.

Another example: You say, "I would like a glass of water."

The person says, "People in Nigeria kill for water, doesn't drinking water make you feel guilty?"

You say, "I would like a hamburger?" The person says, "Cows die so you can eat that hamburger."

I say, "Vegetables feel pain so I think we should all not eat and starve to death so Mother Nature can proceed on its carnivorous killing way without our help."

Here is a blank because I want to know why most people think they are philosophers when in all truth the vast majority of us really don't know squat?

____

____

____

Vent and I were the only customers left in the coffee shop. I had not seen the other people leave. The dog had not moved and Patricia was still reading. Dogs have the ability to sleep 9/10ths of their lives away and feel no guilt. If we did that we would be labeled a manic depressive. Which is better dreaming your life away or working your life away? Circle one: DREAMING... WORKING...and a blank for your reasoning:

____

____

____

A question for those of you who circled WORKING. Did you dream when you were a child about working? YES...NO...

If you dreamed about working and not playing are you an idiot? YES...NO...

If you are an idiot is it people like you that have made the world the way it is today? YES...NO... But to be fair here is a blank to explain your answer:

____

____

____

I dreamed as a child about fishing for trout. It was not until I was older I realized I could have made a living guiding trout fishermen. I could have lived my life floating back and forth on a trout river. River guides are now getting $200 to $400 a day per person which beats the hell out of minimum wage.

Even though you might get rained and snowed on or drown, is being a fishing guide really work? YES...NO...

I must say if I would have followed my dream and became a fishing guide I would not feel the least bit guilty at all about floating down a river while you slaved your life away at a job you do not like.

Depressed about my wisdom coming so late and having not being brave enough to follow my dream I glanced at my watch. It was 9 p.m. I had died some more and I had 13 hours until my plane departs – that is if the plane was on time. Why is it doctors and planes are never really expected to be on time? If they are people exclaim in happiness, "The doctor was even on time," or, "For the first time in my life my plane was on time." If anything thing else in your life was not on time you would be peeved. Here is a blank for someone to please explain why this is. Don't worry your answer will not stop doctors and planes from not being on time.

____

____

____

Vent said to me, "I really don't need any more coffee. I am not hungry and I don't want a beer but a mixed drink would be nice."

I had a strange vision of beer, hamburger and fries, and caffeine churning around in my stomach. It was not a pretty vision but I could see nothing wrong with adding a few ounces of spirits to the mix. "There is a nice bar around the corner," Vent said.

I briefly wondered what a nice bar was to Vent. A nice bar to some people might be a biker bar or a tit bar and to be fair an all male review bar – nice is one of those words that should not be trusted. Do you really trust the word nice? YES...NO...

I went on a blind date once that a friend of mine set up. He informed me emphatically that the girl was **NICE**. I pictured either a Jewish girl or a Catholic girl with a conservative haircut, little makeup, mildly attractive, and shy. The blind date wore black leather pants, a leather vest that barely contained her breasts, she had purple hair, a skull tattooed on her forehead, was built like a lumberjack, and her favorite thing was beating the shit out of men that wore suits or were nice to her. Like I said, be careful about the word nice.

Vent removed his wad of cash, lay another twenty on the table, and we headed for the door. Patricia waved, almost the type of wave a rodeo queen waves as she is riding around the arena while all the cowboys are thinking lewd thoughts about how they would like to rope and tie her up. Question: Do you think cowboys while watching the rodeo queen riding around the arena ever concentrate on her wave? Yes...No...

If they are looking at her wave are they the weirdest cowboys you have ever heard of? YES...NO...

Are cowboys the salt of the earth like country people want us to believe? YES...NO...

If cowboys are the salt of the earth why is there so much domestic violence and racial hatred in the West? Not counting horse thieves, cattle thieves, alfalfa and hay thieves, tack thieves and dishonest sale barns?

____

____

____

There were a few people outside. I figured they were doing what people do in all downtown cities late at night – normally looking for drugs or hookers. There were no police cars. The police being smart enough to patrol the more expensive parts of town late at night where murder, robbery, and such are less likely to happen, and if there is a call to go downtown by the time they get there the perps (police talk) would in all probability be gone, which cuts down on the chance of getting shot.

As we headed to the bar Vent and I did not talk. It would seem that after all the coffee we would be screaming at each other, but maybe coffee effected Vent like giving speed to over active kids, which has always seemed strange to me, why don't they just put the little hyper-active buggers to work? You know – mow the yard, wash the car, vacuum the house, do the dishes, run around the block, clean your room. I hate to sound harsh but it might work. When I was feeling antsy on the farm my grandfather made me muck out stalls, after shoveling straw and shit for a few hours I slept well. Do you think the fact we have so many over active kids is because they sit around on their ass watching T.V., talking on the phone, looking at their ipad, etc. etc.? YES...NO...

Here is a blank if you want to comment:

____

____

____

The bar was clean and simple – notice I did not say nice. There were four men and a woman sitting at the bar and two of the four oval tables had couples. The tables and chairs were oak and matched the bar. In the corner was a dart board, a real one, not one of those plastic boards that make true dart players want to throw up and are illegal in the UK.

In the other corner was a jukebox. Mellow jazz drifted through the room and mixed well with the stale odor of whiskey and beer. No one was smoking so I took it the management was not as lenient as BILL'S BAR. No customer in the bar even glanced at us as we entered, but the bartender, a thin bald man in his mid to late 50's, smiled and called, "The usual dry vodka martini, Vent?"

Vent did not reply but waved as he led the way to a table.

The bartender brought Vent a martini with two olives. I could have saved him a trip if he would have asked me what I wanted after calling to Vent but what the hell, some people like to make things more complicated. "And what would you like?" he asked pleasantly.

"Rum and coke," I ordered, and feeling guilty for him being complicated, added, "put it on the bar, I will come get it."

"Thanks," he replied like he really didn't care if I went to the bar and picked up the drink or if he brought it to the table.

Question: Why do we have the tendency to make things so complicated?

____

____

____

Is it because we don't know any better? YES...NO...

Is it because if we didn't make things complicated we would not know what to do? YES...NO...

Is there anything that is simple anymore? YES...NO...

List a few things that are simple:

____

____

____

If nothing is simple anymore why don't we do something about it?

____

____

____

Vent did not pick up his drink and I gave him a quizzical look. "I will wait for you," he said.

The bartender put my drink on the bar and feeling like a dog fetching a stick I brought it back to the table. "To our meeting," Vent toasted. "I must admit I have enjoyed your company. You have brightened my evening."

"If it would not have been raining so hard I would not have missed my turn. I would be in Phoenix and we would have never met," I said.

"Don't give me that everything that happens in life is destiny," Vent said.

"But maybe it is," I said. "Why else do things happen to people that have no rhyme or reason?"

"There is no rhyme or reason in life. There is no destiny," Vent said. "Everything is random."

"If everything is random it takes the magic out of life," I said.

"Why?" Vent asked.

I contemplated the question but could not come up with an answer.

Do you think there is magic in life? YES...NO...

If you think there is magic in life list a few things that are magical:

____

____

____

Do you think everything in life is random? YES...NO...

Do you think everything in life is destined? YES...NO...

Do you think some things are random and some things are destined? RANDOM...DESTINED...BOTH...

You might have to write a literary novel to try and answer this next question. If you do I hope you have luck getting it published. If no publisher will touch it you can self publish it on Amazon, but let me warn you most Amazon readers aren't really into deep stuff. They are more into zombies, erotica, romances, and mysteries.

Do you think mankind has made up the idea of destiny merely to try and convince ourselves that there is a meaning to life? YES...NO...and a large blank for your reasoning:

____

____

____

I sipped on my rum and coke and came up with a new phrase I could say to people when something happened to them that had no explanation. Instead of saying, "Damn, it was your destiny." I could say, "Damn, blame it on random. That random is a sneaky bastard"

Not wanting to be gender biased I could also say, "Damn, blame it on random. That random is a sneaky BITCH." For the record I am in no way gender biased. I think women should do and be what they want just like men. I do believe that women should get over the strong desire to have children now that we have too many people on Earth. When we have discovered how to leave this planet we are in the process of destroying then women can start craving children again.

Maybe mankind should take ten or twenty years, have no children, and adopt. Is this a good idea? YES...NO...and WHY either way:

____

____

____

For a reason beyond destiny or random I heard a fragment of a conversation two people at the bar were having. The fragment was: "Corporations are people my ass..."

I looked at Vent who seemed to be greatly enjoying his martini, but martini drinkers are like that. "Vent," I said, "What do you think about the Supreme Court ruling that corporations are people?"

"Who are those over educated, bought off, stupid motherfuckers?" Vent hollered so loud everyone in the bar momentarily stopped what they were doing and looked at him, then deciding he was either a nut or a freak, but harmless, went back to whatever they were doing before being rudely interrupted by a hollering man. "Does a corporation eat?" Vent demanded more than asked while waving his arms.

I shook my head.

"Does a corporation fall in love?" Vent asked starting to vibrate.

I shook my head.

Then Vent fired off a blast of questions so quickly I had no time to either nod or shake my head so you can answer them.

“Does a corporation have to shit?” YES…NO…

“Does a corporation get sick and have to go to the hospital?” YES…NO…

“Does a corporation like to have sex even though they like to fuck normal people around?” YES…NO…

“Does a corporation ever go to jail?” NO…

Vent stopped to catch his breath. He started to say something else but I cut in, “I take it you do not think corporations are people?”

Vent nodded his head, which to most people means yes, but coming from Vent I took it to mean, what the hell do you think you dumb ass.

Corporations cannot answer this question. Do you think corporations are people? YES…NO… and WHY:

If you think they are people which one would you like to get naked? There has been a rumor going around that IBM is kinky and a lot of the oil corporations are into orgies and really greasy stuff:

How on earth did the Supreme Court rule that corporations are people? Is it because corporations own them? YES...NO...

Is it because the majority of the judges are republicans and republicans always back big business? YES...NO...

Is it because the Supreme Court judges are idiots? YES...NO...

If corporations are people are 'WE THE PEOPLE' in all truth nothing but corporation slaves? YES...NO...

Here is a question. In our legal system it states that people on trial will be judged by a jury of their peers. If this is true than should white people have an all white jury? YES...NO...

Black people an all black jury? YES...NO...

Every skin tone of people imaginable has a jury of only people of their color? YES...NO...

Poor people a jury of poor people? YES...NO...

Gay people and all combinations of – lesbian – transvestites – etc. etc. juried by people with the same sexual preferences? YES...NO...

Corporations have a jury of other corporations? YES...NO....A blank for your comment on all the above questions:

____

____

____

The bartender came over with two more drinks even though we had not ordered. I suppose we looked thirsty. "Are people robots?" Vent asked the bartender.

"The way we are brainwashed into believing what we believe, and still think that we make our own decisions, yes, we are nothing more than robots," he replied.

"Good answer," Vent said.

"It's the only answer," the bartender said.

What do you think? Are we all merely robots that have been brainwashed into believing what we believe? YES...NO...

If you would have been born in Germany in the 1930's would you have been brainwashed to be a Nazi? YES...NO...

How about if you were born in Iraq? Would you have been brainwashed to be a Muslim? YES...NO...

What if you were born in Rome? Would you be brainwashed to be Catholic? YES...NO...

If you were born in any country in the world would you be brainwashed to be a member of that country? YES...NO...

What if we taught all of our children that we are all a member of one country called the Earth, and we really need to start getting along and solving world-wide problems? Would we then be brainwashed as children of the Earth? YES...NO...

Here is a blank for you to list all the things that your individual country has convinced you, you should believe: I will start: My country is the best.

____

____

____

The fact you were born where you were born and brainwashed to be whatever you are, is that destiny or random? DESTINY...RANDOM...

Vent and I took a drink at the same time – corporations and robots are pretty heavy topics especially since we are brainwashed by where we are born.

There is one statement I hate: "Everything that is supposed to happen happens." I do not believe that war is supposed to happen, starvation, genocide, cancer, and many other things. Do you believe everything that happens is supposed to happen? YES...NO...

How about when there are tornadoes, hurricanes, mudslides, earthquakes, a meteor hitting the planet and killing millions of living things. Are these disasters supposed to happen? YES...NO...

If your answer is YES please explain:

____

____

____

If your answer is NO please explain:

____

____

____

"Vent," I asked, "What do you think about the medical system in the United States?"

To my surprise Vent displayed no outward sign of disgust. He sipped his martini, pursed his lips slightly, and said calmly, "It all depends on whether you are rich or poor. If you are rich you can afford the outlandish health insurance and the impossible to pay medical bills. If you are middle class or poor and cannot pay for a good insurance policy you are in a load of trouble. The United States medical costs compared to other free nations are on the average 50% higher. The United States is the only country in the free world that a private doctor will turn away a patient because they do not have insurance. I am not saying all doctors do, but many."

"What can we do?" I asked.

Vent smiled a distant smile, "Move to Denmark or Sweden or France or England or Canada or Switzerland or any other European country. You will pay more taxes but your medical will be free or inexpensive."

Question: Should everyone in the United States be entitled to health care? YES...NO...

Question: If you are rich do you care if the poor die because they do not have health insurance? YES...NO...

To be fair: If you are poor do you really care if a rich guy with good health insurance dies? YES...NO...

If you are middle class and your wife or husband or child gets cancer and after insurance your bill is $1,127,416 do you think this is right when in Europe (all the countries listed above and others) your bill would top off at around $10,000. YES...NO...

Should health care be a capitalistic enterprise? YES...NO...

Why are people in the United States afraid of socialized medicine?

____

____

____

"I have been in the V.A. since I got out of the army," I said to Vent. "The V.A. is a socialized system. No matter how many bad things have been said about the V.A. it has always been good to me. When I was flush I was on co-pay and when I was broke everything was free. They now have a program that if they cannot get me an appointment within 30 days I can go to a civilian doctor."

"V.A. has been good to me also," Vent said.

Here is a partial list of all the socialized systems in the United States, which I suppose everyone who is against socialism will want stopped immediately.

1) THE ARMED FORCES

2) THE INTERSTATE HIGHWAY SYSTEM

3) FEDERAL WATERWAYS

4) THE FBI

5) BUREAU OF PRISONS

6) CENSUS BUREAU

7) CONGRESS

8) UNITES STATES DEPARTMENT OF LABOR

9) HOMELAND SECURITY

10) HEALTH AND HUMAN SERVICES

11) NATIONAL PARK SERVICE

12) WELFARE SUBSIDIES

13) PRIMARY AND SECONDARY EDUCATION

14) SOCIAL SECURITY

15) MEDICADE AND MEDICARE

16) VETERANS ADMINISTRATION

There are many more. If you are interested do some research? The complete number of socialized systems in the United States might astound you.

The medical industry says they have to pay millions of dollars to develop medicines and that is why in the United States prescription drugs cost more than anyplace else in the world. Seems to me the same pharmaceutical companies sell their pills and drugs all over the world.

Does Europe get different drugs than the United States? YES...NO...

If your answer was NO why does the United States pay the tab for the world? Here is a blank for you to try and explain why: The answer – because we are the wealthiest country in the world does not count because we are not:

____

____

____

How many Senators and Congressmen do you think the medical industry has bought off with their powerful lobby? 2...4...7...15...28...37...283...or all of them. Here is a blank if none of my numbers match your answer:

____

____

____

"If every child after they graduated from high school had to go into the military it would solve our medical problems," Vent said. "They would all be enrolled in the V.A. when they got out."

If you had a child that was 18 years old would you say, "It's time for you to go over to the Middle East and kill as many terrorists as you can. You can put off college for a few years since there are enough college grads anyway. Off you go, write when you have time. Don't worry, it is always the other person that gets killed or has their arm or leg or face blown off." YES...NO...

If your answer was YES...why?

___

___

___

If your answer was NO...why?

___

___

___

All Israeli kids, girls and boys, at 18 years old go into the military. Name a few other countries where military service is mandatory?

___

___

___

Do you think every person that is always clamoring for war should be put in the military and placed in a line unit no matter how old they are? YES...NO...

Many people get disability clauses to get out of the military but they work to make a living. If they work to make a living why can't they work in the military?

___

___

___

Do you think it should be mandatory for any person in any way connected with the government to have served in the military? YES...NO...

"You brought up the last question," Vent said calmly but then yelled at the top of his lungs. "What do you think about the price of college in the United States?"

"Are you sure you want to know what I think," I said, not alarmed at all as I was now conditioned to Vent's hollering.

"No, I asked you because I do not want an answer," he said sarcastically.

"Answer him," all the people at the bar said in unison and glared at me like I was the one that had yelled. A young couple at a table were so in love they only had eyes for each other and did not react to the noise. I had a momentary pang of sadness for them.

Looking back on your life can you define young love? YES...NO...

If your answer was YES will you please write down your definition:

____

____

____

If there is young love is there also old love? YES...NO...

If your answer was YES is old love better? YES...NO...and why?

____

____

____

"Are you going to answer my question or sit there and look like an idiot?" Vent asked.

"The price of college is absurd, more absurd than our medical costs," I said, adding, "I do know I should not have wasted a few years of my life in college because I really had no idea what I wanted to do and I was really not college material."

"College is expensive for several reasons," Vent stated in a voice that was one octave above normal. "One reason is the government knows most people can't afford the cost of college so they give loans to students that generate huge profits for years and years to come. If a student is lucky they might pay off their school loans in twenty years."

Do you think Vent is right? YES...NO...and a blank for your reasoning:

____

____

____

"Another reason," Vent continued, "is by keeping education costs high the vast majority of poor students will never be able to go to college and there will be an endless supply of cheap workers."

Do you think this statement is true? YES...NO...and a blank for your reasoning:

____

____

____

"In the majority of European countries a person that is suited for college will receive a free education. There are also many trade schools for those not suited for college. When a person graduates from the trade school they often times make more money than a person with a college degree," Vent stated.

Why is the United States lacking in trade schools?

Why do we look down on people that go to trade schools when what they do is necessary for a productive society?

Why is it that, when cuts have to be made in state budgets, usually one of the first items to get funding cuts is education?

Is it because the politicians really and truthfully want the majority of people to be dumb? YES...NO...

Education the United States at the moment is ranked 17th in the world. Finland and South Korea are 1st and 2nd and Russia is 18th.

Do you think you are smarter than a person from Finland? YES...NO...

How about a person from South Korea? YES...NO...

I won't even ask if you think you are smarter than a Russian. I will ask if you like Russian Vodka? YES...NO...

If you do, do you like it chilled? YES...NO...

We know Russia wants the majority of their people to be uneducated – after all they are reformed communists? What is our excuse?

Is a democratic person smarter than a communist person? YES...NO...

If your answer is YES tell me what a democracy is. After you have answered look up the real definition and see if your answer is correct:

By your definition is the United States a democracy?

Also, is a democratic person smarter than a socialist person? YES...NO...

If your answer was YES tell me what a socialist is:

"When education funding is cut the state governments also cut lunch programs at schools. It is strange that in America almost 46.5 million people live in poverty and there are over 15 million children that do not get fed on a regular basis. Why do we cut food programs in schools?

____

____

____

Is it right to cut food programs? YES...NO.

If you answered YES have you ever been hungry? YES...NO...

If you answered NO you had better get out and start voting.

We cut lunch programs in our schools but we send money to countries around the world to feed children in their schools. Am I missing something here? YES...NO...A blank for why we do this:

____

____

____

For your information California and Arizona cut funding for education and tripled the money they put into prisons. Does this mean prisoners make more money for the state than smart people? YES...NO...

Does this seem wrong to you or is it just me? YES...NO...

If corporations paid more taxes would the government have to cut education?

YES...NO...

I hate to say this but if the rich are only 5% of the population that leaves 95% of the people that can vote. I am extremely bad at math but 95% voting can defeat 5%. Or am I wrong? Does 95% voting defeat 5%? YES...NO...

If it does you would think we could elect some politicians that really and truly do care for **THE AMERICAN PEOPLE**.

If you circled NO I want to know who your math teacher was?

____

____

____

Or, does the Electoral College really mess up the idea that your vote for the President really means anything anyway? YES...NO...

If your answer was YES then why if the popular vote is different from the Electoral College vote does the Electoral College vote win:

____

____

____

If your answer was NO I do not know what to say.

And, if you really want to know who wins elections look up **SUPER DELEGATES**. Who and what they are might change your beliefs in the United States democratic system. Here is a blank not to fill in but to take the time to research Super Delegates:

____

____

____

"One thing about the United States," Vent said, "grade schools and high schools are free which is no different than anyplace else in the world so there really is no excuse for not at least learning the basics. School systems curriculum, all set by the state, are a little off center though. It might help if there were courses on voting, how to balance a check book, how to apply for a loan, what interest on a loan really means, how to make and live on a budget, how to save money, how to apply for jobs. No time in my life after high school have I ever made use of my ability to diagram a sentence, speak French, or run around a track several times."

Is there something wrong about learning basic life skills in school? YES...NO...

If your answer is NO why don't schools teach basic life skills?

____

____

____

If your answer is YES you probably believe in the statement 'ignorance is bliss'. Which is as stupid as the statements, 'it is what it is,' 'what goes around comes around,' 'you will get yours,' all of which are not true but must mean something to the people that say them about 6,000 times a day.

Do you believe most little quips that are supposed to sound deep and philosophical really have any meaning? Yes...No...and a blank for your deep and philosophical reasoning:

____

____

____

Vent finished his martini. "To sum it up," he said. "College should be within the economical reach of all people that have the ability for college and there should be more trade schools."

"Do you think it will change?" I asked.

"Not the way the country is going," Vent replied sadly. "And not while banks and the government are making millions of dollars in interest on school loans. Students pay higher interest on their loans than corporations or banks when they borrow money."

Is it grand theft for the government and banks to charge almost usury rates for college loans? YES...NO...

Why did the government pass a law that a person cannot bankrupt a school loan? Banks can bankrupt, airline companies can bankrupt, corporations can bankrupt, and Trump does it all the time. A blank if you understand their reasoning:

____

____

____

If you are like me and do not understand their reasoning here is a Question: Why is it the government always seems to steal from the poor and get away with it?

____

____

____

I finished my drink and on queue the bartender came over. "Another round?" he asked.

I shook my head. Vent shook his head, dug out his wad of cash, handed the bartender some money and said, "Keep the change."

"Thank you for the drinks," I said to Vent.

"My new found friend I think it is time for me to go to my apartment and for you to go to the airport and discover what random fate awaits you until the airplane whisks you back to your life in Phoenix," Vent said.

I felt depressed, almost sad.

"Here is my card," Vent said taking a card out of his inside suit pocket. "One day you might visit Kansas City again." The card stated in bold letters. **WRITER OF UNREAD NOVELS AND HATER OF ALL THINGS UNJUST. I DO NOT HAVE A PHONE, iPAD, A COMPUTER, AN E-MAIL. IF YOU WANT TO CONTACT ME WRITE OR COME BY. SAMUEL R. RUTHORFORD JR – 111-A MAIN ST. KANSAS CITY, MO 64112**

I gave Vent my card which did have a phone number and my work e-mail. For some reason the fact I had a phone and e-mail made me feel uneasy? Why, I have no idea?

Is there ever a time that you feel slightly off kilter after you have been on your electrical devices all day, checking e-mails, Facebook, dating sites, bank figures, weather reports, Twitter, Google, etc, etc, etc, and you realize there are many constructive things to do in life that have passed you by? YES...NO...

If you miss a phone call is it really all that important especially since there is a thing called voice mail? YES...NO...

How did people before us get by without all the instant information? I don't know is not an answer:

____

____

____

Now that most correspondence is done by e-mail there will be no old letters from relatives to be passed down from generation to generation – no war letters – love letters – etc. Is this sad to you or do you really care? SAD...DON'T CARE...

I have many old letters from relatives that are over one hundred years old that I cherish even though they remind me that I am nothing but a passing, but, I can't remember the last time I wrote a letter. When was the last time you wrote a true letter? I mean one with a pen or pencil and paper and written by hand where you had to address an envelope and all that labor intensive stuff like attaching a self adhesive stamp. Here is a blank if you can remember the last time you wrote a letter. Put the approximate date and to whom the letter was written:

____

____

____

Do you think writing letters is important? YES...NO...and why either way:

____

____

____

There is a company in California that writes hand-written letters for corporations, businesses, and private individuals. The owner started with two employees writing letters and now has over fifty. Her client's state people receiving hand written letters feel special and it cheers them up.

Would you rather receive an e-mail Christmas card or a Christmas card in the mail? E-MAIL...CARD IN THE MAIL...

Would you rather receive a hand written letter or an email letter after the death of a loved one or friend? E-MAIL...HAND WRITTEN LETTER...

Do you think hand written letters have more feeling than e-mail letters? YES...NO...

This has nothing to do with writing letters but with the world's dependence on electrical devices what would happen if all the electricity went out? CHAOS...MASS CONFUSION...and a blank for your thoughts:

____

____

____

"I have another question," I said to Vent. Before I left I wanted to know more about Vent the man than his opinions.

"One more and that's it," Vent said.

"Were you ever married?" I asked.

Vent's eyes softened and seemed to look through me, as if he was savoring a thought or vision from the past. I was immediately sorry for asking the question. "It is really none of your business," Vent said quietly, "but I will tell you." He then paused and took a deep breath before continuing. "I met Ann in college. She was not a beautiful girl but I am not a handsome man. Until her I had never really had any interest in being with a woman. After the war I was trying to find myself and not doing a very good job of it. Ann was in the library and for a reason I do not know I asked her if she would like to go to a movie. The rest was history. I was not smitten, nor did I fall so deeply in love I could not eat, but she made me smile. To Ann there was always a good side to everything and she believed that given time all things will turn out for the good. She was my friend and confidant and a candle in my dark world. We were comfortable together and were married by a Justice of the Peace. At first we did not want children but when we did it was too late. After eight years of marriage Ann died from breast cancer. I have dated a few women. I have women I enjoy being with. But I have never met another woman that is my deep friend. To me friendship is more important than love. But with Ann she was my love and my friend."

"I am sorry," I said.

"Life is seldom kind," Vent said as he stood.

Do you believe friendship is stronger than love? YES...NO...and why?

____

____

____

Is your partner, either gay or straight or in-between, your true friend? YES...NO...

Can you tell your best friend more things than you can tell your significant other? YES...NO...and why?

____

____

____

The bartender was busy mixing drinks and did not wave goodbye.

Outside neither of us said anything for a few moments. "I live that way and your car is the other way," Vent said breaking the silence. "Do you think you can find your car?"

"Daniel Boone and I are distant cousins," I replied trying to be funny and hide the sadness I felt at leaving.

"I'm glad I met you," Vent said with a genuine smile. "I wish you the best in your life and hope you realize at least one of your dreams."

"And you too," I said.

We shook hands. Without another word Vent turned and walked away. He was no more than twenty yards from me when he started waving his arms up and down concerning a topic we had not discussed. I felt left out – almost abandoned. I watched him until he went around the corner. I had the urge to run after him. I wanted to talk more. I wanted to try and solve the problems of the world. I took one step toward the corner, but I stopped and glanced at my watch for no reason. It was exactly 11 p.m. My plane was supposed to depart at 10 a.m. I had 11 hours to go – somehow it seemed ironic – 11 p.m. and 11 hours. Feeling slightly sad and ironic and reminded once again I am dying I headed for the rental car.

Have you ever felt sad and ironic at the same time? YES...NO...

If you have was it a weird feeling – one that cannot really be explained? YES...NO... And a blank if you can explain it:

____

____

____

A few people hurried by me to wherever they were going. A car sped by. The driver was a shadow that I would never know. The rumbling of the car echoed off of the mute brick buildings. Much to my relief the rental car had not been stolen. Besides being known for its barbeque Kansas City is also known for a higher than normal amount of car thefts. I could see myself explaining to the car rental agent how I got lost in downtown Kansas City and was forced to spend many hours drinking, eating, and conversing with a man and that is why your car was stolen. Of course, I did not buy any extra insurance, and did not know if my insurance covered the theft of a rental car. The wonderful world of insurance, but on the other hand if there was not insurance then there could not be the lucrative market for insurance fraud, which many people pull off very successfully for many years – the mob is especially good at it and truthfully, I hate to say this, it is really not that hard to have cars, boats, travel trailers, motor homes, etc. etc. get seemingly stolen and collect insurance. How many of you have scammed an insurance company? Here are three answers – circle one: I HAVE...I HAVE NOT AND I AM FIBBING...I HAVE NOT AND I AM TELLING THE TRUTH...

Do you think people who scam insurance companies are low-life scum bags? YES...NO...

Or are the insurance companies low-life scum bags when they do their very best to pay as little as they can on any legitimate claim – especially medical insurance claims? YES...NO...

About to get in the rental car I looked at the spot where I had first seen Samuel R. Ruthorford Jr. rushing by and waving his arms in the air like a mad man and I smiled. "You are one sorry bastard," I said filled with admiration.

In your life has there ever been a person that was a sorry bastard but you still held a deep fondness for them? YES...NO...

If your answer was YES here is a blank to explain why:

____

____

____

If your answer was NO, you don't need a blank, but, to not offend you I will give you a blank anyway:

____

____

____

I headed north on Interstate 35 and the exit to the airport. I would return the car, take the shuttle to the airport, and wait for random fate.

I do not like to wait. I can say that now, but when I was in the war waiting for the helicopter to come in and pick us up and fly us out to the field, I wished I could have waited forever. But, that is a different kind of waiting.

Do you like to wait? YES...NO...If you do why?

____

____

____

If you don't why?

____

____

____

The interstate was busy – mostly big trucks roaring to one part of the country to roar to another. They reminded me of primeval beasts with no conception of time and without beliefs. Question: If mankind had no beliefs or could care less about time would we be classified as beasts? YES...NO...and a blank:

____

____

____

Or, are we beasts and our conception of time and our beliefs are really nothing but bunk? YES...NO...and a blank.

____

____

____

Do you think elephants or monkeys or any other animal which we have labeled as beasts really care that they have never read a book? YES...NO...

Would beasts have invented weapons of mass destruction? YES...NO...

Do you think if the roles were reversed between beasts and mankind the beasts would enjoy blasting us to death with large caliber rifles and putting our heads on their walls? YES...NO...

And on the topic of beasts do animals have souls? YES...NO...

How about jellyfish? YES...NO...

Did dinosaurs have souls? YES...NO...

How about your pet dog or cat or fish or bird or lizard – you know one of those animals you love. Do they have a soul? YES...NO...and a blank to explain your answer.

____

____

____

And, do they love you? YES...NO...and of course a blank:

____

____

____

The Pope said pets will go to Heaven. It made me wonder what happens if a pet owner goes to hell? How long will it be before the pet finds another owner? Circle your answer: 100 YEARS...1/3 of ETERNITY... 3 DAYS...THE PET WILL STAY BROKEN HEARTED FOREVER.

Years ago while trying to find my inner self by ingesting things only primitive people living in the jungle should I thought a rock loved me. I had a most in depth conversation with the rock. After declaring my love for the rock I put the rock in my pocket so we would never be apart. Two days later when I was about to do my laundry I found the rock, wondered what the hell a plain brown rock was doing in my pocket, and tossed it in the alley. I will not even ask if any of you have ever been in love with a rock. I know there are a lot of old hippies that are in love with trees and bushes and rivers but those things are different than rocks. (Disclaimer: Don't tell any rock what I said.)

There were two other people on the shuttle bus from the rental car lot. None of us looked at each other either out of fear, apprehension, or the fact that close to midnight on a bus headed for the airport is not the greatest place to start up a conversation. Question: Would you say hello or how are you to a stranger sitting on a shuttle bus going to the airport late at night? YES...NO...and your reason:

____

____

____

I checked my bag and cleared security. When I have to fly I do not wear a belt. I wear slip-on shoes. Have no change in my pockets. Only carry my identification, credit card, and a little cash in my inside jacket pocket. If I carry on a small bag that will fit under the seat I have no toothpaste, clear liquids, jelly, toast, peanut butter, apple butter, in my carry on. If I am asked why I am flying, even though I like to fly, I tell them because I missed the train. I hate to say it but the majority of the TSA people that I have been around would not know what to do with a real terrorist if they saw one. Also, I don't think it is possible to stop all attempts to blow up planes. Question: Can all attempts to blow up airplanes be stopped? YES...NO...

If your answer was YES here is a blank to explain how:

____

____

____

If your answer was NO there is no need for a blank.

I know one way, everyone stop flying. But then the terrorists would start blowing up trains, busses, boats, donkey caravans, camel caravans, bicycle groups, blimps, you name it.

I headed to where my plane would depart in 10 hours. I passed a bar that would stay open until 2 a.m. and had microwavable sandwiches. About a dozen people were drinking and watching TV, a few were intently studying their laptops, several were talking into the type of cell phone that plugs into your ear and gives robots complexes. The combination souvenir, magazines, and assorted junk food store was closed. I supposed people don't read late at night and don't want a T-shirt or pink teddy bear with Kansas City embossed on it. Three fast food establishments were closed, which was too bad as some over cooked greasy chicken really sounded delicious. A chain coffee shop was closed. A shoe shine stand with seats for three people was shuttered up. There was a young couple at the gate, cuddled up in the corner on the floor trying to sleep. The sign stated Flight 714 for Phoenix would be boarding at 10 a.m. I had a choice, I could try and sleep or go to the bar – sleeping was out as I still had at least 240 grams of caffeine blasting through my veins. I suppose I could also walk around the airport, but walking around an airport is not exactly like taking a stroll in a park. I did wonder why, when airports are open 24 hours, there was not at least one fast food joint open. One time I was in the Seattle airport late at night and everything was open. Go figure. The clam chowder was very good and the fried fish as good as any I ate by the pier. They also have a great Chinese restaurant. Do you think at least one fast food joint should stay open for 24 hours at an airport? YES....NO...

If your answer was YES here is a blank to list what fast food joint or joints you would you like to see stay open?

____

____

____

I sat at a corner table in the bar with my back to the wall. It made me momentarily feel like a rich gangster but even I know the gangster life is not like TV shows or movies. I suppose if you like the idea of getting shot or going to jail it would be a good life or if you are just lazy and don't want to get a real job. I do know that a high ranking gangster that has killed fifteen people, smuggled drugs, and other crimes can now snitch all his friends, not go to jail, and get a TV gig.

Is this right or wrong? RIGHT...WRONG...

Feeling like doing a good deed I went to the bar as I did not see a waitress and only one bartender. The same beer I drank at BILL'S BAR was on draft for seven dollars, which was high but not as bad as beer at the Phoenix airport which is nine dollars.

I suppose there is a hidden tax that is added onto booze in airports that we don't know about, or the owners of airport bars are a group of greedy capitalists who have the chance to pillage the public and do. They are also too cheap to hire extra help.

Do you think that many stores and businesses limit the hours of their staff so they don't have to give them benefits? YES...NO...

How about the pizza guy that does commercials with famous football stars, lives in a multi-million dollar mansion and pays his people minimum wage? Do you think if he paid higher wages it would change his life style? YES...NO...

Do me a favor and boycott his pizza establishments. There are a zillion small pizza shops trying to make a living that need your business.

Merely for fun do you think Warren Buffet is really a nice guy? YES...NO... He did have his picture taken with Sir Paul McCartney and lives in Nebraska.

Beer in hand I returned to my table and glanced at my watch, yes, as always, I am closer to dying. It was almost 1 a.m. in the morning. The last two hours had gone by to wherever time spent doing nothing goes to.

Have you ever wondered what you could have done with all the wasted time you have spent during your life - time watching TV - time sitting in a car going to and from work. Time at a job you hate. Time dreaming about doing something you would really like to do and then never doing it? If you add wasted time onto time that we spend sleeping there really isn't much we do with our lives. Question: Is it selfish to do what your mind tells you, you want to do with your life? YES...NO...

I do know some people live their life doing what makes them happy. I also know most don't. Why do we spend most of our time doing what does not make us happy?

____

____

____

Are we afraid? YES...NO...

Are we stupid? YES...NO...

Do we say it is our duty? YES...NO...

Wouldn't the people around us be happier if we were happy? YES...NO...

Do people drink too much and do drugs because they are happy? YES...NO...

Do people drink too much and take drugs because they are unhappy? YES...NO...

If money made you happy wouldn't you think most businesses would be overjoyed to pay their workers more? YES...NO...

If your answer was YES why don't they?

____

____

____

If your answer was NO you must be a distant cousin to the Walmart family and I bet it was your idea to cut out the elderly door greeters to save money. Good for you I hope you are proud – let them eat cake and all that.

Question: Does anything really ever change? YES...NO...

I think we need more caring in the world and less profit margin. Do you think we need more caring? YES...NO...or is profit margin all that really counts? YES...NO...and a blank for your reasoning for both questions:

____

____

____

Here is a question that is not as confusing as it sounds. Can there be caring while still being concerned with profit margin? YES...NO...and a blank:

____

____

____

The beer tasted good. Maybe I should go on a cheap beer, cheap hamburgers, several mixed drinks, and coffee diet. Since I am in my late 60's how long do you think I would live if all I did was drink beer, booze, coffee, and eat hamburgers. Circle one: 5 MORE YEARS, 8 MORE YEARS, 10 MORE YEARS, 0 MORE YEARS...and a blank if you think none of these are right:

____

____

____

There was an ex-slave that lived to be 112 and lived on whiskey and beans. When he was young most drinking water, if it was not made into beer or hard liquor, was not fit to drink. There was a disease from bad drinking water called cholera that killed a lot of people in the good old days.

Cavemen lived an average of 38 years. They lived in a non-polluted environment and ate only organic food. Am I missing something here? YES...NO...

I was studying the way the bubbles at the bottom of the beer glass were systematically making their way to the top when a shadow settled over the table. I had a quick thought that maybe in all truth Batman was real, but when I looked up it was not Batman, but a medium height, slightly plump, jovial looking guy, in a rumpled suit holding two beers. "I don't feel like drinking by myself," he said. "Would you mind if I joined you?"

In all truth I wanted to be alone with my weird thoughts but I replied, "Sure, have a seat."

I suppose there is always a small portion in most of us that really doesn't want to offend people. Do you think this is TRUE or FALSE?

The man seemed genuinely happy to have company. His smile made me smile. Genuine smiles are like that, contagious sneaky little bastards that want you to feel happy when in all truth you don't feel happy at all. Question: Are you happy? YES...NO...

If YES why are you happy?

____

____

____

If your answer was NO why are you not happy?

____

____

____

Are there more happy people than sad people? HAPPY...SAD...

Are there more happy people than depressed people? HAPPY...DEPRESSED...

At times I wonder what happy means. To me it is equal to or more confusing than love. I will not ask another question about love as there is no one, nobody, who can answer the question of what love really is. If you understand love I urge you to write a book. The book will sell at least two billion copies to all the lonely people in the world and make you a very rich person. Then you can write another book on how money did not really make you happy but it sure made it a lot easier to exist in this world. You will then fall into the one percent group, and the majority of people will hate you, but you really won't care if they hate you or not. Is this true or not? YES...NO...

"My name is Henry Jackson," the man said as we shook hands. Since I felt Henry Jackson would not be like Samuel Ruthorford Jr. and think my name was undignified I said, "My name is William," and kept it at that.

What is a last name anyway? I mean who really cares if your last name is Smith, Peters, Jones, etc. etc. Do you care what a person's last name is? YES...NO...and why?

____

____

____

What if your name was like the Brit's and French aristocracies that are about eight names long? Would you care if people remembered them all? YES...NO...

The original Native Americans had the naming process down. You were named after an object. For example: Flying Hawk, Big Bear, Running Elk, Soaring Eagle, Fast Antelope, Sunrise, Full Moon, etc...etc...

There were also Native American names that did not make the history books: Mouse Face, Skunk Head, Crawling Coward, Elk Droppings, Vulture Beak, Sagging Tits, to name a few.

Do you think all Native Americans before the white man were good people? YES...NO...

Do you think that there were a few Native Americans that were ass holes? YES...NO...

If there were no bad Native Americans there goes the idea of KARMA once again.

Henry Jackson did not offer me one of his beers. "What do you do?" Henry Jackson asked me, which I have stated before is a question I do not like, but in our modern society means everything to most people, depending on your answer you will either be praised, shunned or all manners of in between. I am a doctor always gets a look of admiration. I am a writer gets a look of confusion unless you are famous. I am a drug dealer either gets you a look of hate and contempt or a lot of admiration (sometimes more than a doctor). I work for the city gets a nod. I drive an over the road truck gets you a look of sympathy and advice on what hemorrhoid ointment works the best.

If you say I am a good person, with a good heart, and I try to help as many people that are less fortunate than I am, most people will look at you like you are some kind of weirdo that should see a shrink.

I decided to tell Henry Jackson the truth about what I do. "I sell cars," I said, adding, "I have decided that even though cars are the biggest reason we should not breath the air, and are causing the ozone hole at the top of the Earth to try and get the hell out of here, it is a good job and will not get me thrown in jail."

"Interesting," is all Henry Jackson replied, which made no sense to me as selling cars is not really all that interesting. But what the hell do I know? Here is a blank line for you to list a few things that you find interesting: You cannot list politics, religion, or anything about the opposite sex:

____

____

____

"And what do you do?" I asked Henry Jackson although I really didn't care. I do know if I was in prison and asked that question I might get stabbed for not minding my own business. How I know this is none of your business.

“I am a criminal defense attorney,” Henry Jackson replied with no airs or pretension, unlike prosecuting attorneys that always seem to come off like they are related to God and all they care about is justice.

Do you think that prosecuting attorneys main thought is justice? YES...NO...

If you answered YES why is it that most Prosecuting Attorneys after several years of getting to know the judges start their own Criminal Defense Attorney firms?

____

____

____

Is it because criminals that may or may not be guilty pay better than the government? YES...NO...

Is it because the Prosecuting Attorney’s know that in all truth they could give a damn less if a person is guilty or not guilty, they only want convictions for their resume? YES...NO...

Is it a crime that most criminals have more money than hard-working lower and middle class people? YES...NO...

And to be fair most high ranking criminals have more money than many of the upper one percent, who, not implying guilt without proof, might be big criminals who hire big time defense attorneys that were once prosecuting attorneys, and now know all the judges and can get them a light sentence or probation.

Question: Do you think legal big business is any more honorable than illegal big business? YES...NO...

Would you trust Donald Trump? YES...NO...

Would you trust George W. Bush? YES...NO...

Would you trust anyone on the Supreme Court? YES...NO...

Would you trust Obama? YES...NO...

And just for the hell of it would you trust George Washington? YES...NO...

Or good old Thomas Jefferson who liked his slave women a little too much? YES...NO...

"What do you specialize in?" I asked Henry Jackson.

"Mostly drug cases," he said.

"Lucrative," I said as a statement not a question.

"Very," he replied as a fact.

"And why, for no other reason than conversation are you in the airport in Kansas City at such a late hour?" I asked.

"I'm headed back to Chicago. I lost a case today. Guy got busted for the third time with a small amount of pot and he got twenty years." Henry Jackson said without remorse.

"People get less time for manslaughter or armed robbery or rape," I said.

Henry Jackson shrugged his shoulders.

If you live in Missouri and smoke weed I would get the hell out of there as fast as you can. There is something about the Bible Belt that is not very forgiving. Why is this? A blank for your answer:

____

____

____

Is it because God likes to see people in jail? YES...NO...

Do you think twenty years for pot is right? YES...NO...and your reason:

Here is some information which many of you might not know. There are many crimes that now have mandatory sentence limits. A judge can only sentence a person by what the law mandates. Judges don't like the law as it gives them no latitude for sentencing. Years ago in the wonderful state of Texas, Blacks and Mexicans caught with small amounts of marijuana were given 15 to 20 year sentences. This was because the Texas prison system is based on huge farms and they needed labor to run them – still true to this day. It is strange that the United States is the most incarcerated country in the world. We even beat China and Russia. Are you proud that we are the most incarcerated country in the world? YES...NO...

Do you believe there is liberty and justice for all? YES...NO...

Do you think people that commit crimes that do not involve weapons should be given a break the first time? YES...NO...

Do you think we have too many laws? YES...NO...

Do you think marijuana should be illegal? YES...NO...

I really don't know of any old hippies that have started crime syndicates or murder for hire organizations. Seems to me making drugs illegal has caused a lot of crime syndicates and murder for hire organizations that if you owe them money will kill your wife, kids, grandmother, goldfish, dog, brother, sister or distant cousin.

Do you think all drugs should be legal and drug addicts treated like the sick people they are? YES...NO...

Here is one for you. Heroin in this country has never been so cheap or in such quantity. Production in Afghanistan has tripled. Do you think it is strange that since we have spent zillions of dollars fighting drugs in this country and zillions of dollars helping the Afghans that there is more opium and heroin on the street? YES...NO...

Do you have any idea how the heroin is getting into the country in such huge quantities?

____

____

____

Terrorist's groups all over the world mainly get their money by cultivating and distributing illegal drugs. If drugs were legal how would they make their money? Would they start a chain of day care centers? YES...NO...

Would they beg countries to make something illegal so they could continue blowing people up? YES...NO...

What do you think they would do?

____

____

____

Here is a little known fact. The Coca Cola Company is the only company in the United States that has the legal right to import coca leaves. They import over 100 tons of leaves a year that is sent to the Stepan Company for processing. The processed cocaine, around 300 kilos, is then sold to Mallinckrodt Incorporated in St. Louis to be used for medical purposes. The Mallinckrodt Company also imports opium from India. Do you think the medical industry uses 620 pounds of cocaine a year? YES...NO...If your answer is NO where does all the legal cocaine go?

It is a known fact many doctors and nurses do partake in the cleanest cocaine available.

Here is something to think about. Every city in this country has a poor side of town. According to many of our esteemed politicians the reason most of the people on the poor side of town can't get a job is because they are lazy. Are drugs kept illegal mainly for the fact the government really does not want to help those with little choices and they know the only way for poor people to exist is by selling illegal drugs? YES...NO...

Does drug use affect Wall Street? YES...NO...

Has drug use affected Hollywood? YES...NO...

Does drug use really affect the country? YES...NO...

If your answer was YES does alcohol use really affect the country? YES...NO...

How about addictive over the counter pain medications? YES...NO...

Did you know that more people die from over the counter pain medications than all illegal drugs combined? Why is this? I have ruled out the fact the people who die cannot read the warning label, but maybe this is true in states that have cut money for education.

Another tidbit of information, more people also die from infections they catch while staying in a hospital than from all illegal drugs.

I have it in my will if I get sick and can't communicate I want to be taken care of in a barn with cows and goats around me that a big drug syndicate has used to stash large quantities of narcotics.

Should prostitution be illegal? To be fair I am talking about male prostitutes, female prostitutes, and gay and lesbian prostitutes. YES…NO…

It does not seem to have harmed Germany or many other countries. Why does it harm the United States but not other countries? A blank for your answer:

____

____

____

Henry Jackson finished one beer and started on the other one. In my mind a defense attorney should be a scotch on the rocks type of guy? Do you think defense attorneys are the beer type or scotch on the rocks type? Circle one: BEER…SCOTCH… and a blank to write down what you think they would drink if you think neither one of these is right.

____

____

____

To make sure and not have an attorney sue me for being prejudice what would a female defense attorney drink?

____

____

____

What would a defense attorney (male or female) who is a minority drink?

____

____

____

Any combination of races that were defense attorneys (male or female) what they would drink?

____

____

____

Just to be safe I will ask what would a defense attorney of any race, gender, combination of races, either on this planet or any planet in the known and unknown vast expanses of space drink?

____

____

____

I signed a contract once with the phrase, "known and unknown vast expanse of space," in it and still got screwed.

Warning!! Never!! Never!! Sign a contract that offers you a part of the net. There will never be a net – slick lawyers make the net vanish into thin air. Tell them you will take a part of the gross. There is always a gross.

A man was recently fired who was president of a large sports organization. He was fired because he said that a certain female athlete "hit like a girl." Women all over the country went nuts at such a terrible and demeaning statement. Question: This is for sports that have anything to do with hitting – example: golf, tennis, baseball, football, softball, racquet ball, squash ball, volley ball, boxing, cage fighting - here is a blank for you to add any other sports you can think of that I have missed that concerns hitting:

____

____

____

Now I will ask. Do the majority of girls hit the same as men? YES...NO...

Would a woman or girl be offended if someone said "They hit like a man." YES...NO...

What if a girl said to a man "you hit like a girl?" Would men start protesting in the streets? YES...NO...

Who would win if women boxers fought men boxers? MEN...WOMEN...

Who would win if a women's soccer team played a man's soccer team? WOMEN...MEN...

Who would win if a women cage fighter fought a man cage fighter? WOMAN... MAN...

Do women hit like women? YES...NO...

Can a pro lady golfer hit a golf ball farther than a pro man golfer? YES...NO...

Forgive me but I think girls do hit like girls for the main reason they are girls. For all you girls out there that feel like you are really men I apologize. For all you men that feel you are girls the answer is a little trickier. Circle your answer. Do you men that feel like you are a girl hit like a MAN or a GIRL?

Is this man woman thing getting a little absurd? YES...NO...

I think it is time for women to start holding doors open for men. What do you think? YES...NO...

If the genders are supposed to be equal than let's be equal. I also think that women should ask men out and pick up the tab. What do you think? YES...NO...

And it should be women that have to ask men if they want to get married. YES...NO...

I do think it is a crime that women do not make the same money as men. This is not true for men and women working for minimum wage.

Question for men only. Are you glad you are a man and not a woman? YES...NO...and a blank for your reasoning:

____

____

____

Now for women. Are you glad you are a woman and not a man? YES...NO... and a blank for your reasoning:

____

____

____

And to be fair for gay people here are two questions. Are you glad you are a man that is a woman? YES...NO...and a blank for your explanation:

____

____

____

Are you glad you are a woman that is a man? YES…NO…and a blank for your reasoning:

____

____

____

For you people that do not know what you are – either a man or a woman – I really don't have a question for you. Sorry, you are on your own.

"And why are you sitting at an airport late at night?" Henry Jackson asked me.

I told him the complete story from my grandmother's funeral, to missing my plane because of a storm, and meeting Samuel R. Ruthorford Jr. – alias VENT, and as many of the topics Vent and I discussed that I could remember.

When I finished Henry Jackson gulped the rest of his beer, gave me a strange far away look and without saying goodbye, adios, see you later, nice meeting you, or any other parting remark scurried away as if I had bad breath. To be redundant it was fine with me as I really wanted to be alone anyway. I could have said when he asked to join me, "No, I don't want any company you rude fuck. Don't you know in this modern world we are all paranoid and it is instilled in us from the time we can crawl to never trust a stranger except at Halloween? Now get the fuck out of here."

After a few minutes I started thinking how vastly different my feelings about the country and the world have changed since I was young. When I was young there was, even amongst the turmoil, a sense of hope and a belief mankind would work things out. Now there is a sense that mankind will never work things out. Maybe it is just me getting old and cynical. What do you think? Do you think mankind will get together and work things out or will it only get worse? YES MANKIND WILL or NO MANKIND WILL NOT…and why:

____

____

____

Do you think God or Buddha or Allah or any other deity that is defined by any and all different religions will appear in the sky and say, "All right boys and girls, enough is enough, good guys you line up over here, bad guys you line up over there," and all the bad guys will be destroyed? YES...NO...

I did not finish my beer but headed slowly to the gate. The few people I passed were nothing but faceless images. I felt empty, confused, dejected, lost, and even with an overdose of caffeine still pulsing through my veins, tired. For a reason beyond my understanding I saw Vent's face and my Grandmother's face in my minds eye. They were talking to each other, smiling, and seemingly having a grand old time. How can anybody in this world sit back and have a grand old time? A blank for you to explain to me how people have a grand old time:

____

____

____

Chairs in airports are not meant to be slept in. Why, I don't know? By the number of flights that are cancelled, overbooked, or delayed you would think they would be. None-the-less I slept like, to use an over used phrase, a log, even though the statement, "I slept like a log," really makes no sense. To my knowledge, limited as it may be, logs do not sleep. If you believe logs do sleep please do not write me a letter, email me, or contact me on Facebook and tell me how unfeeling I am to the plight of a log, or tell me if I have wooden furniture, a wooden fence, or anything wooden that I am part of the reason mankind is destroying the Earth. To be truthful I don't think hugging a tree will change the fate of trees. Even though I do feel the destruction of our natural forests is a crime. Do you think there are better building materials than wood? YES...NO...

If you do what are they?

____

____

____

I seldom sleep without dreaming. I wish I did. My dreams have no pattern to them and make no sense. They bounce around in my not so resting brain like the ping pong balls in the lotto machine. When I woke up people were lining up for the flight to Phoenix. My first thought was I had died and gone to hell. The terminal was a moving mass of humanity. Even though every bone in my body ached from sleeping in a chair my biggest desire was to brush my teeth, but keeping with my normal ability to go through life never prepared, my toothbrush was tucked safely away in my suitcase, which I hoped was now in the cargo hold of the airplane. Glancing at my watch, yes I have died more, the flight still had over twenty minutes until departure, and since I was flying cattle call airlines with no set seating assignments and was in the last boarding group I rushed to the gift shop and bought a package of gum, dashed to the bathroom and splashed water on my face, stuck three pieces of gum in my mouth, and darted back to the gate feeling surprisingly refreshed.

In line to board I had the urge to forget Phoenix and go find Vent. I felt like I was leaving something important behind, something that would change my life for the good if I only embraced it. It was with a heavy heart I handed the smiling gate attendant my boarding pass: goodbye new life – goodbye – goodbye. Why is it the majority of people will stay stuck in a trap and not take chances?

___

___

___

Is it because we think we are the only person that will live forever and in time we will outlive our chains? YES...NO...

Is it the retirement carrot that is dangled in front of our noses that many government officials are trying to extend until one is 70 years old? YES...NO...

Even though the seats are too small, the majority of the people are annoying, there always seems to be a crying baby, and the drinks are overpriced, I do enjoy flying, it always fills me with wonder looking down at the Earth. I always think about the thousands of people below, each with their own opinions, each with their own wants, needs, and desires, and I feel about the size of an ant's foot. I was sad thinking I would never see Vent again. Even if I wrote he would not write back. "I wish you well Vent," I said to the Earth below. "Live long and prosper."

The flight attendant stopped by my row. She looked tired. "How much longer before you get some rest," I asked.

"My last leg is Phoenix."

I ordered a Bloody Mary. After the drink was delivered I read the on plane magazine – a zillion ads for Las Vegas, a list of great steak houses around the country, adds for golf courses that cost more to play than the average man makes in a week, retirement communities if you have several million dollars to spend while you are dying, a letter from the president of the airlines guaranteeing his airline will never charge for baggage, vibrating chairs that will take all your cares away, cheap cigars, clothes and shoes for big and tall men, suitcases if you plan on living on an airplane, travel routes all over the country, an article about a famous singer that I thought was dead, a guy selling bow ties, and various other topics that are of interest only to bored people whose main concerns are if the plane is going to get blow up by a terrorist or hit a storm and they will puke for the next few hours. Did you know that flying is the safest way to travel? YES...NO...and that the odds of getting killed in a plane crash are six million to one.

The lifetime odds of a person dying in a car crash are one in four hundred and seventy.

Seems to me we should be deathly afraid to drive or ride in a car. Is this true? YES...NO...

This plane landed safely in Phoenix. I was home or I should say I was where I presently live, but I did not feel elated or relieved to be back in Phoenix. I felt more like a stranger as the crowd of airport humanity rushed by me. I said to myself, "We are all in a hurry to die," and headed for baggage claim.

As I watched the baggage carousel go in its endless circle I felt sorry for it. Are we like a baggage claim carrousel always going in an endless circle? YES...NO...

Or maybe life is going in an endless square? YES...NO...

Or maybe life is going in an endless triangle? YES...NO...

Or maybe life doesn't know where in the hell it is going? TRUE...FALSE...

If you know where life is going here is a blank to explain where. If you have an answer would please message me on Facebook and tell me where life is going. I have no idea.

____

____

____

I grabbed my bag, got on the bus for long-term parking, and within twenty minutes, and minus fifteen bucks a day parking fee, I was on my way to my apartment. I had a passing thought about my grandmother and for reasons beyond me I wondered how many people would come to my funeral. After several moments of deep thought I figured only the preacher and decided I will give my body to science with one stipulation, there has to be a tag on my toe stating, "Have fun. Life is short. Capitalism might not be the answer. I regretted many things during my life but now that I am dead I regret nothing."

Question: Will you regret anything when you are dead beside the fact you might not be in Heaven. YES...NO...Here is a blank to list what you will regret:

____

____

____

The weeks passed and life went back to its normal routine. Get up, coffee, shower, cuss my way through traffic, sell cars, lunch, sell cars, cuss my way through traffic back home. But there was one major change, I was selling more cars than I ever had and I didn't in anyway deceive any customer. I tried to place the customer in a car that suited their needs, not their wants, and I tried to get them the best deal that I could – being honest at first was difficult but it made me feel good. My commissions weren't as big as they could have been but they were enough. I think the change in me was caused by my conversations with Vent, especially the story of his wife and the way he used his money to help people. I was convinced mankind should try and be good with or without God's help.

Does there have to be a God offering salvation for man to be good? YES...NO...

Would God refuse entrance to Heaven to people who had been good their complete lives even though they professed they did not believe in God? YES...NO...

Months later I was standing on my back porch admiring the view of Picacho Peak as the sun was setting. There is something about a cactus studded rocky hill that reminds me life is both tenacious and precarious at the same time. Several birds were singing back and forth to each other and I realized it was May. Winter was over, which is a funny thing to say when you live in Phoenix. The fact it was late spring left me feeling out of touch. Time had passed without me realizing I was dying. Lord, I need a bigger watch, one that counts months. Don't ask me why but I walked to the corner convenience store to buy a newspaper. I had not glanced at a paper in months and had never really watched the news on TV as my shift at the car lot got me home after the news. That can be a good thing or a bad thing. Is it a good thing to not watch the news? YES...NO...

Is it a good thing to not know what is going on in the world? YES...NO...

Does it make any difference if you know what is going on in the world anyway? YES...NO...

Do you really give a damn what is going on in the world? YES...NO...

Do you care that the Dallas Cowboys once again might blow their chances at making the Super Bowl? YES...NO...

Or the fact that over 50 percent of all women actresses in the movies have had nose jobs and breast implants? YES...NO...

I bought a newspaper and a quart of cheap beer. All you craft beer experts can look at me in disgust but I don't care. I also bought a bag of salted peanuts. I know salt is bad for you but unsalted peanuts to me are like non-alcoholic beer – PLEASE?

Back home and after reading several articles in the paper my mind erupted with an image of Vent. His silver dollar eyes were bugging out of his head. His arms were flapping up and down like a hummingbird on speed. He was having difficulty breathing. I read about terrorist attacks in Spain, France, Belgium, England, Afghanistan, Iraq, Iran, Syria, and several countries in Africa I didn't even know were countries. Israeli soldiers killed several Palestinians because the Palestinians killed several of them. The police in Albuquerque, New Mexico over the last four years had killed 26 unarmed people. Four cops had been killed in various places in the United States. According to a top Republican climate change is not real. The United States was catching hell about killing people that were American citizens that had turned into terrorists and wanted to come back to America and kill Americans. The ocean had almost more plastic in it than fish and on and on and on and on and on and on and on and on and on and on and on and on.

Is there ever a stop to the insanity? YES...NO...

Do you have a friend that owns an island, preferable in a warm zone that would let me move there and grow organic vegetables? YES...NO...

If your answer is YES you can e-mail me and I promise not to tell where the island is.

I jumped out of my chair, ran to my computer, and wrote Vent a letter. No need to inform you about the majority of the letter, but the essence of it was I missed talking to him and I was sorry for not writing sooner. I also mentioned I needed some of his advice on what he thought about the recent world developments. I did not mention that I really didn't think advice would help.

I drove the letter to the post office – afraid the mailman might lose it.

Have you ever written a letter that was so important to you, you drove over ten miles to drop it off at a post office instead of merely putting it in your mailbox? YES...NO...

Life went on. I once again started watching the news and reading the paper. I followed various political organizations without taking sides. I joined Facebook, Google Plus, Linkedin, and other social media groups and was overwhelmed with postings of cats, dogs, young ladies throwing the world the finger and showing off their cleavage, men in provocative poses for women, gay men wanting to get married, God is good and will save the world, protests for and against every political party in the country. I read the opinioned pros and cons on every topic one could imagine. So many pros and cons I started wishing I had been born in Denmark – supposedly the happiest people in the world. Question: Would you like to live in a country that is the happiest in the world even if it is cold most of the time? YES...NO...I would give it a try but sad to say I could not afford the airfare.

If you hated summer would you live in Saudi Arabia if it was the happiest country on Earth, which it is not? YES...NO...

Most of the middle-eastern countries are not known for being overly happy or even remotely happy – they are well known for ignoring human rights, graft, and stifling women. But, it can be said they are extremely good at getting the United States to send them money and fight their wars for them in exchange for a few oil leases.

Question: Saudi Arabia has the biggest army, more weapons, more planes than any other country in the Middle East yet they are not involved in any fighting against any terrorist organization. Does this seem strange to you? YES...NO...

Could it be Saudi Arabia backs the terrorists? YES...NO...

Bin Laden was from Saudi Arabia.

I started missing Vent's blasts at our modern world and I wondered once again why I was drawn to him. The feeling was like when I was a kid and my relationship with my little brother, who I could not stand most of the time, but when a bully picked on him I did my best to knock the bully's teeth out, who for some reason was always bigger than me.

Now I like my younger brother but I will never forgive him for sneaking into my room and breaking all my model airplanes. This question is for older brothers only. Did your younger brother ever sneak into your room and break your things and you still protected him? YES...NO...

Did you ever beat the crap out of him and tell him if he ever came back in your room again you would rip his nose off of his face? YES...NO...

And if you did punch your younger brother were you then smacked by your mother or father for picking on somebody that was not your age. YES...NO...Their reasoning being, your younger brother broke all your things because he was merely expressing his frustrations in the only way he knew how, which, I will say, is pure bullshit. My younger brother was a sneaky little shit head that would grow up to be a very wealthy CEO that never gave me any stock tips. That will teach me to be a protector and punch guys twice my size for picking on my brother. All I can say is it was a good thing I was a fast runner when I was a kid and it could be one reason I always seem to be slightly paranoid.

More time passed and besides selling a lot of cars in my effort to seal the fate of the ozone layer a nice thing did happen to me. I met Julia. I truly enjoyed being with her and she enjoyed being with me. We both had been dumped by our spouses. She had two grown children, who to my relief, all live on the East Coast. I hoped we would grow to love each other. I still had thoughts about Vent and wondered if he would ever answer my letter, which, down deep I doubted. Do you think that Vent will take a few moments and answer my letter? YES...NO...

Would you answer a letter if I wrote you? YES...NO...

I hope so.

Is it rude to not answer a letter? YES...NO...

Several more months went by to wherever months go to when they are used up and waiting to be reincarnated for the next year. Reincarnated is not the correct word as they come back the same. January is still January, February is still February, etc. etc. I have always thought it would be a good idea if every year we had twelve completely brand new months. Not the same January, February, March, etc. etc. It could be Harold, Bill, George, etc. etc. or whatever a special elected committee wanted to name them for the upcoming year. New Year's Day would then be a completely new beginning, not the normal and boring January 1st. What do you think? Would a brand new year every year give you a better attitude leading into the New Year? YES...NO...

Or would many people get so confused they would forget what month it was? YES...NO...

Learning twelve new things for a lot of people each year might be a little too much for them to take.

It was a Saturday morning, one of the few Saturdays I was off, Saturday and Sunday being the best car buying day of the week. Mr. and Mrs. can come to the car lot together. If they have kids they drag them along. While Mr. and Mrs. are looking at the cars they are trying to figure out how they can afford the payments and still eat or buy clothes for the kids. But according to a previous beloved President of the United States, "Ask not what the government can do for you but what you can do for the government," means pay more taxes, work harder, get paid less, fight useless wars, don't care if our bridges are wearing out, our highways are in lousy shape, you can't afford to get sick, everything costs more although wages have not risen. This statement was made by a man who never really had to work in his life and spent most of his time sailing, whoring around with starlets, and getting shot up with speed. Don't get me wrong, they are not reasons he should have been shot, but maybe, just maybe, it is also the job of the government to help some of the people and not our job to take care of the government. Do you believe it is our job to support the government? YES...NO...and why?

I had not checked my mail in a few days which is normally only bills, advertisements for cheap insurance, credit card companies wanting me to sign up with usury interest rates, grocery store advertisements, and an occasional flyer for a new dentist who would take x-rays of my teeth and clean them for an introductory offer of only $1,500. I was surprised when going through my mail there was a letter from Samuel L. Rutherford Jr. I looked at the letter in disbelief – almost shock.

If you answered YES to the question when I asked if Samuel L. Ruthorford Jr. would write me back you are correct – sorry there is no prize only the inner joy of being right.

I was both nervous and happy as I opened the letter. Samuel L. Ruthorford Jr. used monogrammed stationary and the letter was written in handwriting that years ago would have made a writing teacher proud. I read:

Dear William:

I received your letter several months ago and am glad all is well with you. I want you to know I enjoyed our brief time together, it is nice to vent with another person and not alone, although I do not care if people think I am crazy or not. Through a twist of the randomness we exist in I will be in Phoenix over the holidays (Christmas or whatever else you want to call it) if your biggest problem in life is what people call the holidays you must have it good or you are stupid. It would be my pleasure to get together and vent over topics that our too short time together made impossible to cover. There is no need to write back. I will give you ample warning as to my arrival. I would appreciate it if you contacted your Sheriff Joe Arpaio and inform him I am not a Mexican so there is no need to illegally harass me when I come to Arizona.

Sincerely,
Samuel L. Ruthorford Jr.

P.S.

What do you think about ISIS?

And, Atlanta, Georgia just passed a law that you cannot eat and drive at the same time.

I see some school districts are trying to ban books.

The private prison system is getting out of hand.

What do you think about people that don't give their children immunizations because they think diseases have taken a vacation?

How about plastic pollution filling the ocean?

What do you think about super delegates?

Do you think all Muslims are bad people?

Do you think all Christians are bad people?

I have more things I want to vent over but I detest long letters.

Sincerely once again,

Samuel L. Ruthorford Jr.

The letter made me smile. Vent's P.S. list did not. Even though Vent said there was no need to write back I did:

Dear Samuel L. Ruthorford Jr.

Looking forward to your visit. Will give Sheriff Joe the wrong dates when I know you are visiting but, be sure to carry your I.D. even though by law you do not have to. To add fuel to the fire I have a few questions for you.

As always, your random friend,
William Brown

To be continued

VENT BOOK TWO WILL BE RELEASED BY OPEN TALON PRESS IN 2017

If you enjoyed this book would you please leave a review on Amazon or any of your favorite reading sites and tell 45,000 of your friends to buy a copy. Thank you for your time.

You can view Robert K. Swisher Jr's many other novels on: swisherbooks.com.

www.ingramcontent.com/pod-product-compliance
Lightning Source LLC
Chambersburg PA
CBHW082101090726
47910CB00008B/2552

9780997909609